SUSSEX
HORRORS

STORIES OF
COASTAL TERROR
&
OTHER
SEASIDE HAUNTS

HERBS
HOUSE

Published in Great Britain in 2018 by Herbs House
An independent publishers

1

Layout and cover design by Mark Cassell and Redski Redd

Published by Herbs House

ISBN 978 0 9930601 5 1

Printed and bound for Herbs House

First Edition

This anthology is for all those who
like to be beside the seaside,
beside the sea ...

SUSSEX
HORRORS

CONTENTS

SEAGULLS

Rayne Hall

While the stencils dried above the dado rail, Josie squatted on the carpet, eating her first breakfast in the new studio flat.

Three seagulls stood outside the window, white-feathered and silver-winged, their eyes yellow halos around death-dark cores. Every time Josie lifted a spoonful of muesli to her mouth, their greedy stares followed her hand.

According to the *Welcome To Sussex* pamphlet, European herring gulls were an endangered species, worthy of protection. On the brochure's cover, seagulls looked so pretty: white-feathered, silver-tipped, soaring serenely in an azure sky.

In close-up reality, they were ugly, unromantic beasts, from the wrinkled flat clawed feet and the grey-pink legs to the folded wings ending in feathers like black blades. Each thumb-long beak had a hole in the upper half, some weird kind of nose she supposed, a gap through which she could see the misty sky. Then there was the red, a splash of scarlet on each beak, as if they carried fresh innards from a slaughter feast.

A sudden screech, and they dropped their pretence at peacefulness. Big beaks were pecking at her miniature roses, ripping them out and apart, tossing green fragments.

Josie stormed to the window, waving the tea towel like a weapon. Three pairs of wings unfolded, filled the window, lifted off. Screeches of outrage tailed off into the distance.

Of the pretty pink roses she had planted with so much care yesterday, only stems and shreds remained. With delicate fingers and tender words, she pressed the roots back into the soil and gave them water to settle back in.

She returned to work, sponging the next layer of stencils, delicate blooms in pink which would go well with chiffon curtains.

~

At noon, she left the stencils to dry and prepared lunch - muesli again, since she had not had time to stock her cupboard.

The gulls were back. Sharp bills pointed at the muesli on her spoon, begrudging her every bite. The one with deep grooves on its chin knocked its beak against the window. *Tap-tap, tap-tap.* more fiercely: *klacketeklacketeckacketeklack.*

The oat-flakes stuck dry in Josie's throat.

The tallest of the gulls, with head feathers standing up like a punk's haircut, tilted its head back and trumpeted a shattering scream. *Kreeeeee! Kreeeee!* The white chest vibrated with screeches which could have brought down the walls of Jericho. Josie wasn't sure if the window glass trembled, but the shudders in her spine were real.

The gull closest to her had obscene red stains on its beak, like a vampire's bloodied lips. Josie tried not to look, but she had to. Their closeness sent chills up her back, even with the transparent safety of double-glazing shielding her from predatory beaks.

If only she had curtains in place, preferably something as thick and solid as the garish seventies drapes she'd left behind in the shared London flat.

The red-billed gull unfolded its wings, increasing its size to fill the large frame, and more. Josie ducked behind two unpacked suitcases, but still their stares followed her. The studio flat, which had appeared so spacious when she had first viewed it, now closed in on her.

Living by the sea had seemed such a good idea, especially in St Leonards, where the streets hummed with history. She had pictured herself in a dress of sprigged muslin, strolling along the promenade on the arm of a Mr Darcy. A grey bombazine gown and a Mr Rochester would be good, too.

The gulls clucked like hens, trumpeted like elephants, screamed like pigs at slaughter, the noise shrilling through the window-glass and echoing in the unfurnished room. Why had they sought her out?

She scanned the houses on the other side of the road, Regency terraces with elegant wrought-iron balconies and bow windows on pale, ornamented façades. No unwanted visitors plagued those windows, although some seagulls socialised on distant roof gables and chimney pots.

Josie thought of squirting them with water from the plant mist spray, but living in cliffs, gulls were used to splashes, and of pelting them with hazelnuts from the muesli box, but they might just let the missiles drop off their feathers and gobble up the food.

Resolutely, she pulled her floaty velvet coat from a suitcase and threw it full force against the window. The big gull stepped back and dropped off the ledge, but within moments it was back.

Josie retreated to the windowless bathroom, where she emptied a jar of perfumed crystals, a farewell gift from her flatmates, into the steaming tub. Like always, the scent of lavender soothed her. During the hot soak, she was able to view the seagulls' behaviour as a mere annoyance, and her own reaction as ridiculous.

How strange that the birds homed in on her, and how strange that she was so frightened of them. After all, they were only birds, kept out by a double panel of solid glass.

But then, she'd always been frightened easily. As a child, she feared the neighbour's dogs, just because they were big and fierce looking, while young children patted them with fond trust. She could not bring herself to go near the farmer's cows, or the ugly looking turkeys in the cage. All harmless animals, of course, and only a stupid child would be afraid of them. The other kids made fun of Josie's fears, teasing her without mercy until she despised herself.

She covered her legs in thick soapy foam and shaved them with deliberate slow strokes, a reassuring routine, and stayed in the bath until she had used up all the boiler's hot water.

By the time she had rubbed her skin dry, the gulls had departed, probably to the beach to snatch snacks from unsuspecting tourists. In the bright sun, the glass showed zigzagging white lines where beaks dribbled, and white faeces gleamed on the windowsill ledge.

With the monsters gone, she browsed the mail order catalogue for curtains and furniture, designing light-filled, romantic space with swathes of chiffon and Regency prints, and pondered what to wear when she started her new job on Monday.

During supper – more muesli – the same three gulls returned. *Klacklack klackeklack*. All three, hammering against the glass. Josie recognized the grooved throat, the blood-stained beak, the punk-style feathered head.

They knocked the window by moving their heads forward and back. Even ghastlier, the small one kept the tip of its upper beak glued to the glass, and vibrated the lower one. The whole pane rattled in an angry staccato. Josie had heard that bridges collapsed when a unit of soldiers marched in synchronised steps. Would the window break under the persistent pecking?

For the first time, she wished she was still in London, in the soulless grey tower block with views of other soulless grey tower blocks, in a flat furnished with someone's hideous nineteen-eighties leftovers, with flatmates whose unwashed dishes stank up the kitchen and whose stereos thumped through the night. The flatmates would know what to do, or would at any rate drown out her fears with their loud laughter and roaring rap.

"Oh, go away, go away!" she shouted at the beasts. Without the slightest shift of a leg, blink of an eye, twitch of a wing, they sat and stared.

She grabbed a fistful of muesli. "If I give you this, will you go?"

Kreeee-kreeeeeeee. Kreeee. Impatient foot-tapping, as if they knew what was in the box.

She turned the squeaking handle, tilted the window, and dropped the muesli on the sill. They snatched the crumbs as soon as they fell, three scimitar-sharp beaks devouring the raisins and oat-flakes faster than she could dip her hand back into the box. *Kreee-kreee.*

If she gave them enough to fill their stomach, they would not bother hanging around. She grabbed another fistful and pushed her hand through the gap.

Pain shot like a piercing nail through her flesh.

She pulled her hand back, slammed the window shut and twisted the lock. Dark red blood streamed from the wound, dripping thick blotches on the pristine white windowsill.

The gulls yelled in angry triumph.

Having neither antiseptic nor a first aid kit, Josie rinsed her hand under the tap and wrapped it with an embroidered handkerchief. She needed allies, someone who had experienced this kind of harassment and knew what to do. But she had not yet introduced herself to her neighbours, and the harridan in the flat below had complained about the noise of Josie dragging suitcases up the stairs.

Dusk descended, but the gulls did not retire to roost.

Klackedekackedeklcackedeklack, they hammered at the window. Josie blessed the double glazing. Even if they cracked one pane, the second would resist, wouldn't it?

Josie scanned the other buildings in the evening mist. No seagulls were attacking the mock-Georgian retirement homes, the Victorian gothics, the concrete monstrosities from the seventies. Why had they picked her?

Maybe because she was at home when most residents were out at work. Maybe the absence of net curtains had lured them with a tempting view inside. Maybe they'd tried all the other windows, and learnt that they'd not get fodder there. She cursed her weakness of giving them muesli. Now they would not go away.

A soft, prolonged scratch. And another.

One gull was scratching along the edge of the window; the other two pecked at the putty that held the glass in the wooden frame. Josie had heard that great-tits and other songbirds sometimes nibbled at window-frame putty because they loved the flavour of the linseed oil it contained. Since seagulls didn't eat putty, what was their plan? If they pecked the stuff to loosen the glass from its frame, she would be trapped in a room with three violent seagulls hacking their beaks at her. What then?

Klackedeklack.

With her pulse thumping in her throat and ears, Josie put her door on the latch, and tried the flat next to hers, and the ones above, but nobody replied. The flats on the ground and first floors were still unoccupied after refurbishment. That left the one on the floor below.

Josie knocked and waited. A toilet flushed inside. At last, the door squealed open. "You." The sharp-nosed woman, with grey hair clinging like a steel helmet to her skull, stabbed a finger at Josie. "Do you know what the time is?"

"I, ahem ... I know it's late, but ..."

"Nine o'clock. Nine o'clock, do you hear?" Her voice whined like a dentist's drill, shrill, painful, persistent. "A time when decent people expect to be left in peace."

"My name is Josie Miller. I've just moved into flat six." Josie held out her hand.

The woman kept one arm locked across her chest, and with the second led a cigarette to her mouth for short angry puffs. "This is a respectable house. Or it used to be, until they refurbished and let the riffraff in."

"I assure you, I'm respectable, Mrs ..." When the harridan did not supply a name, Josie said, "I'm a PA secretary at Lloyds TSB Bank, and the letting agent has my references. I'm sorry to bother you, but there are herring gulls by my window."

"In case you haven't noticed, this is the coast. Gulls live here."

"I'm just wondering how to treat them. I know they're a protected species ..."

"Pests, that's what they are," the woman snapped. "Vile vermin, so don't feed them. Now excuse me. It's nine o'clock, and decent people have a right to peace."

The door clicked shut.

Josie checked her watch: eight forty-five.

~

She had to build a barrier. If she had furniture, she would push it in front of the window, and if she had tools, she would nail her blanket across. She managed to stand a suitcase on the inner windowsill, balancing her rucksack on top of it, filling the gaps with her still-wet towel and her winter coat.

Unless she held her hand very still, the pain was burrowing through her flesh. Holding the sponge for stencilling would be difficult tomorrow.

At least she no longer had to see the gulls. She lay on the carpeted floor, wrapped in her blanket, fantasising about a four-poster bed hung with drapes of rose-pink satin.

Klackedeklack. Scraaatch.

She turned on her CD player to drown out the seagull sounds. *Thada-thada-doum-thad.* The steady beat gave an excuse to her racing heart.

From below came outraged banging. The neighbour disapproved of the music. Josie plugged her ears with the iPod, but for once, the audio recording of Pride and Prejudice failed to absorb her. The fear in her stomach kept rising to her chest and throat, and she lay awake for a long, long time.

~

On waking, Josie's head ached and her throat scratched with thirst. She groped for the familiar lamp switch, and found only rough carpeted floor. Ah, yes, the new flat, and St Leonards, and the new job which had come up so suddenly.

Her brain felt like it had been boil-washed and tumble-dried. She stretched her aching limbs, scrambled up and stumbled to the window to pull the curtains back and let the dawn light in. No curtains, just a suitcase. Now she remembered: Seagulls.

When she undid the knotted hankie, she found the wound already healed over, the only slight discomfort coming from the tightness of the encrusted skin.

She lifted the suitcase away from the window. Sunlight bathed the room. Outside, cool dawn changed into a golden morning, and the distant sea sparkled like diamond-sprinkled satin. Nobody had ever been killed by a wild bird. A breath of the fresh, salt-laden morning air would drive the last of the childish scares from her over-tired head.

On the other side of the road, three white-feathered, silver-winged gulls sat squatting on chimney-pots, haloed by the morning sun, a picture of romantic innocence.

Josie turned the squeaking handle and threw the window wide open.

They rose, fluttered, soared ... and then they were upon her.

THE STEALTH OF SPIDERS

Jonathan Broughton

The motor on my mobility scooter whines. Come on! Come on! I urge. The concrete ramp isn't steep; the surface isn't bumpy. It's the length; one switchback after another. I've seen roads like these on telly, zigzagging up a mountain.

I can't think that the 'Mobility Access' for Bulwer-Lytton House, a twenty-storied block on the Hastings Estate is the next best thing, but it feels like it.

The top, at last, and I trundle towards the square-shaped door. I'm panting, which is mad; it's the anxiety and I reach for my inhaler.

Tilda's voice echoes in my head. *Abigail, if I see your bitch-face anywhere near my flat I'll tip you out of that scooter, tie you up and leave you to die in a cupboard.*

Charming, coming from my sister! What a pity you're dead, Tilda. Now you won't have that pleasure.

The metal entry pad beside the door is just within reach, though I have to stretch to press some of the higher numbers. The lock clicks and the door opens an inch. I ram it with my scooter and it swings wide. I accelerate into the hall before it has a chance to bang shut.

The air stinks of chemical lemon and the lights buzz. The bright bulbs make me squint. They sound like angry flies. A web hangs in tatters off one of the plastic ends. Did the spider think a fly was trapped inside?

I check my watch. Daylight is fading and I want to be gone before night falls. I'm vulnerable out alone in the dark in my scooter. I offer up a silent prayer: Please let the lifts be working. Please!

My prayers are answered, the metal doors open with a clang and I reverse the scooter. *Beep, beep, beep.* Floor seventeen. Some of the buttons are smeared with chocolate; seventeen, thank goodness, is clean. I think it's chocolate. Trust Tilda to live in a dump. She always looked immaculate, always lived in a filthy mess; like a spider's dirty nest.

The lift rises with a lurch and a rattle. There's a grey web in the bottom corner where the doors slide open. No sign of the spider. I wonder if it's the same one that spun the web on the light?

With an abrupt jump, the lift slows and my stomach turns over. The doors judder open and I trundle out into a long corridor. The lights aren't so bright, in fact some of them are broken, and the smell is of old things that need a good airing. I follow the numbers on the doors. Tilda lived at sixty-four. I pass in and out of light and shadow and I fancy that when I wheel through the dark bits there is something, or some things, scuttling along beside me. When I pass under the lights that are on, there is nothing there.

Number sixty-four is at the end of the corridor and sharp right, just beyond the stairs. I reach for my bag in the scooter's basket, unzip the interior compartment and take out Tilda's keys. Oh the joy! I can almost see the engagement ring. It *will* be mine again. I quiver at the thrill of anticipation and imagine Tilda's fury and chuckle.

How ironic that Martin gave me the keys; that pale contrite face of his as he begged me to begin the task of emptying the flat. He didn't know who else to ask, he said. "Please help me; after all, you were sisters." I let him grovel, but of course I agreed. I was always going to, because once he loved me. Odd marks covered the backs of his hands, like red pinpricks, but when he saw me staring he slid his hands under the table.

I unlock the Chubb and then the Yale. The door handle feels sticky, though there is nothing obvious smeared on my hands. I push the door open and steer the scooter into the flat. The dry air smells stale and musty. The light switch gleams white, but when I press it nothing happens. Damn! Is it the bulb, or is the electric off? I should have brought a torch.

Another door beside me is closed. I push it open and see the dull shine on a ceramic washstand and, in the corner, a toilet. There must be a pull cord and I wave my hand in slow circles where I think it might be hanging. My fingertips brush against a taut string and I slide them down till I reach the cold smoothness of moulded plastic. I grip it and something darts against my palm and wriggles over my fingers. I gasp and let go and I think, it's hard to see, that the outline of something black runs behind the toilet.

I hate the dark and snatch at the swinging cord and pull. It clicks and clicks again, but the light doesn't come on. I back out of the flat and into the corridor. My heart is racing and I fumble for the inhaler in my coat pocket and grip it tight. I make myself breathe, in and out, slow and deep. Being in the light helps.

I need to adapt my strategy to these new circumstances. Tilda's electric is off and I didn't bring a torch. I can't leave the flat door open and use the spill from the corridor light because somebody might see and come in.

Perhaps I should come back tomorrow? Or perhaps I should switch on my scooter light? It drains the battery and limits my time, which is a pity because I wanted to enjoy picking over Tilda's possessions and now I shall have to move fast.

My heartbeat is calmer, my mind made up and I switch on the scooter light and re-enter the flat. This time I shut the door behind me. Coats hang from a single row of hooks. A white shiny mac with gold buttons hangs from a hanger. It was the one Tilda wore the most and in the gap at the neck, perched on the hook-tip, is a woollen hat with gold and silver flecks. It might almost be hair, or matted web.

At the end of the hallway is a closed door. I'm looking for the bedroom, but this opens into the lounge. Strands of dust brush across my face. Is it dust — for it clings to my skin and when I wipe it away it leaves my fingertips feeling gluey?

Before me, where the light hits, black leather shines with a dull sheen. A three-seater sofa, the black leather such an obvious choice for a slut. A scarlet throw is draped along the back and in the scooter's light, that makes such weird shadows, I imagine it might be Tilda reclining, watching, smirking. I wipe such nonsense out of my head. That was then when she was alive, her vindictive nature exploding into fury when I achieved something that she hadn't. She hated that I was crippled, hated the shame she imagined was pointed at me, at her. We never got on.

The arm rest of the sofa is faded to grey, like the cobweb in the lift and I fancy I see a drawing back of long legs as they arch out of the light, though when I stare, all is still.

I leave the door open and aim the scooter sharp right down the second part of the hall. There is a door on the right hand wall and another at the end. Both closed.

The first is the kitchen, the size of a walk-in closet. My stomach tingles with excitement. The door at the end must be the bedroom and I feel sure that this is where I shall find the ring.

My neck tickles and I flick the skin, but now my mind is racing, set on the imagined joy of being re-united with that which should be *mine*.

"Marry me," Martin had said as he slipped the ring onto my finger. I had burst into tears. My first proposal by a man I loved and the rush of excitement overwhelmed me. I told all my mates at the supermarket where Tilda and I worked and introduced him after a shift, showed him off like a prize exhibit. This is my man, look at me, aren't I clever. A wry smile creased Tilda's lips.

She was jealous. The warning signs that I was too dumb and too in love to notice, hinted that she might be spinning mischief. Not one proposal had ever come her way, though her fame as a man-eater was legendary. That her younger wheelchair-bound sister might claim that trophy first, dripped like poison into her warped mind.

She ensnared Martin with the ease of practised experience, he didn't stand a chance and neither did I.

I threw the ring back at him and two days later saw it glittering on Tilda's finger. I called her every name under the sun, shouted obscenities about her in the staff canteen, texted lewd gossip to her mobile. I lost my man and my job.

Then, a week before her wedding, Tilda died. She wasn't ill, or injured, or murdered. Her heart just stopped. Grim satisfaction at this unexpected twist alleviated my grief.

I didn't want Martin back, soiled goods. Once we had something special and the ring represented that wonderful time, a precious memory that I didn't want to forget.

I turn the handle and ram the bedroom door open. A waft of Tilda's jasmine perfume lingers. In front of me is a double bed covered in a pink satin quilt. Its raised pattern, edged in silver, is of an enormous web. Typical of her cheap attempt at style.

On either side of the bed are two white tables. Against the wall to my right stands a large white wardrobe with golden knobs. One of the doors is mirrored. On the floor is a cream carpet which matches the curtains, which are drawn.

Strands of silk sway and glitter over everything.

My heart is pumping with excitement. I manoeuvre around the bed to the left hand table. This must be Tilda's side because a circular lace doily covers the table's surface. I snort, as if something so delicate made the bitch more feminine.

The backs of my hands and the exposed skin on my face prickle as I blunder through catching wisps of web. I am feverish with anticipation and pay no heed to this minor annoyance.

I wrench the drawer open and tip the contents onto the duvet. I sift through the tubes of moisturiser, most of them squeezed and curling, the opened tissue packets, the small scent bottles. The ring isn't here. There is no jewellery here at all. There must be a box, a special place where she kept her gaudy trinkets. Three of the scent bottles are unopened and I toss them into my scooter basket.

The obvious place to look is the wardrobe. I execute a tight three-point turn. The motor whines and the light dips. The battery metre reads half-full, so why is the scooter straining? The wheels are in shadow and yet, as I shift backwards and forwards, I catch a glimpse of a grey and tattered lump wound around one of the axles. I reach down and shudder at the soft yielding wad that might be an old cloth or … I don't know what, for I toss it away. It hits the floor and bits break off and scatter under the table and under the bed. I don't get a clear look, but they are black and big. It's just my eyes playing tricks, the light, and a naughty child's mix of fear and excitement when they know that the place they are in is out of bounds.

I make my slow way round the bed to the wardrobe. The sensation of passing through taut threads increases. I wave one hand before me and when I reach the wardrobe, two of my fingers are snared as if bound by tape so that I have to spend several minutes rubbing them free. I curse the time wasted and blame Tilda's shoddy housekeeping skills for allowing so much filth to accumulate.

The light bounces off the wardrobe mirror and gives the room a grey aura and in its reflection, darting in and out of the shadows, dropping from the ceiling, moving faster than my eyes can focus, I imagine a swarm of activity around me. Yet when I turn to look, I see nothing, just the glimmer of silken threads.

I fling the wardrobe doors open. The rail is stuffed with clothes. Shoes stand two deep on the floor. A set of shelves occupies the right-hand side that reach the height of the wardrobe. And on a middle shelf is a large red velvet-covered box. The ring must be here. I draw the box out, set it on the bedside table and lift the lid.

I shriek and jump back in my seat. The unexpected tinkle of a music box bursts into tune. When at last my breathing returns to normal, after two puffs of the inhaler, I laugh at my stupidity. On and on the music plays and now that the shock has passed, I find it comforting. And, in the middle compartment of the top tray, is my engagement ring.

Tears prick my eyes as I pick it up and slide it onto my finger. A Swarvoski Crystal on a silver band. It flashes and sparkles, even in this dim light. I feel relieved, content, whole again. "You see, Tilda," I spit. "He proposed to me first, *me*. And this ring proves it."

My scooter light flickers and for a brief moment I am plunged into darkness, before it steadies and shines clear. I must go, but first a quick rummage through Tilda's wardrobe.

I ignore the shoes, I've no use for them. The jeans are far too narrow and I push them aside to get to the tops and the blouses and the dresses. I yank them off their hangers and throw them behind me onto the bed. I'll take more care about what I really want when I get home. Satisfied that I have as much as I can manage, I reverse away from the wardrobe.

The scooter light dims, flickers, goes out. Oh, Christ! I bump the bed and the engine whines as I fumble for the neutral button. The music box tinkles its repetitive tune. Only the curtains, glowing with the last of the daylight, offers a lighter shade in the darkness.

My hair, my face and the backs of my hands quiver as if they are alive, independent of my thought or will. My lips are sticky, smeared it seems with glue, and it is an effort to force them apart. With a touch, light as a feather, I experience what feels like a bulbous body squeezing itself into my mouth and I gag as I choke it out.

The scooter light slowly builds. It is very weak, but I hit the drive button. My eyes hurt from staring so hard and I am sweating. I call for help, but my breathing is too ragged to find the power I need.

The engine growls, sputters and winds down. The light dips, though now that the engine is dead it wavers with the faintest beam. It shines upon the satin duvet and there, in the shadows just beyond the beam's reach, sprawls my sister, Tilda.

The clothes that I threw from the wardrobe lie in a jumbled heap that should mean nothing, yet they shift and pulse as if filled with life, and the shape of Tilda's body in the garments' haphazard arrangements is unmistakable. The light does not reach her face, yet two eyes glint in the dark. They stare, unblinking, straight at me.

My heart hammers in my ears and tears stream down my cheeks. "I'm sorry, Tilda, I didn't mean to come. Martin made me. Let me go. I promise I won't come back."

I see, in my mind, the vicious grin as the corners of her mouth rise. Her sharp voice echoes in my head, though I question my sanity: *I knew you would come.*

My sight is blurred by tears and the strands of twinkling silk that thicken with sickening speed. My upper arms are bound against my chest so that my hands no longer reach the scooter's handles.

Black shapes dart before my eyes and my skin pricks with pin sharpness.

The scooter light dims and goes out. Against the window's outline, there rises from the bed in disjointed jerks, Tilda's head, body and then her limbs, so many limbs, which arch higher than her shoulders. She darts towards me, looms above me. I cannot shut my eyes, web glues the lids back. I cannot scream, for my nose is stopped with silk and my lips are sealed tight.

I hear her laugh, or is it the music-box winding down? I cannot tell. I cannot think. I cannot know. Tilda pounces. Dry dust, musty and rotten, is sucked into my lungs. My chest tightens as if squeezed by many arms and in my head, I scream.

THE REBIRTH

Mark Cassell

Kelly placed the mug of hot chocolate on the table and scowled at the front door. Who the hell was knocking at this time of night? Tomorrow was Monday, when she'd have to face a class of ten-year-olds; right now, she just wanted to relax.

Again, two knocks.

And, why weren't they ringing the doorbell?

"Hang on, for bloody hell's sake," she whispered. Pulling her cardigan tight, she walked to the door. Her bare feet shuffled across the carpet.

The wooden panel was cold on her cheek as she squinted through the peep-hole. A magnified circle of gloom revealed only the neighbour's door across the hall. No one was there. Although having lived on the sixth floor for the past two years, she hadn't really spoken with any of her neighbours. Certainly, there was the occasional exchange, brief and polite, though often forced on her behalf. Never had any come to her door, nor she gone to theirs.

Nope, definitely no one out there.

She unfastened the security chain and opened the door. She thought she heard something out in the hall, something flapping, but the chain rattling against the wood obscured whatever it was. Cold air blew into her face as she peered around the frame and her breath made a cloud. Someone had evidently left a window open in the hallway. The other three doors were closed. No more sounds, if she had indeed heard anything in the first place.

There had definitely been a knock. Twice. Two raps, both times.

She went to close the door and saw a wooden egg on the mat. It was about the size of a typical chocolate egg, yet carved from solid wood. It had to have been a neighbour. She picked it up. It was cool to the touch and pretty weighty, carved with an impressive weave of vines and leaves. Intricate, not one part of it the same, and clearly handcrafted. No way was it machine made.

She closed the door with her hip, without taking her eyes off the egg. Beautiful. Without a doubt, she would take it into class tomorrow. She'd organised for the kids to make their own eggs based on things they love. This was her first Easter as a qualified teacher, and she was looking forward to seeing their efforts. Already, she suspected what some of the children would make. There'd be Star Wars characters, superheroes and villains, and Pokemon, for sure.

She stood the egg upright in an empty glass she'd left on the table earlier that morning. It made a perfect stand.

Why would a neighbour have given her the egg? She went to the window and looked out, wondering if she could possibly see a friend who'd given it to her as a prank. She could only think of Liz, who'd always been the joker. Maybe it was her.

Clouds, like phantoms, streaked the night sky that stretched downward to touch the knife-edged horizon of the sea. Further to the west, Hastings Pier clawed out into the still expanse of water. A twisting row of streetlights illuminated the winding road where a couple of cars shot past. Several pedestrians dotted the promenade. Some hand in hand, others alone.

It wasn't the view that she was interested in.

Closer to her block of flats, the orange haze of a nearby street lamp flooded the area below. A lady stood beside a dog as it pissed up against the car park wall, and further along, through a row of winter-stripped trees, a man wearing a fisherman's cap shuffled past. He was more a silhouette in the gloom of the alleyway. For a moment, it looked like something fluttered in the bare branches above him, shifting with the shadows. Perhaps it was a late-night seagull.

Kelly allowed the curtain to fall back in place.

Back on the sofa, after a quick glance at the egg, she lifted her mug and took a sip. The hot chocolate slid down her throat, energising her taste buds. Where did the egg come from? The remainder of the evening, she watched TV. A half-arsed effort where she kept thumbing the remote. Her gaze repeatedly wandered over to the egg.

Soon, her eyelids drooped and she fell asleep.

~

"So," Kelly said, having waited for each child to sit in their seats, "all your eggs are in, and waiting to be judged."

The room of twenty children sat alert, eager for the winners to be announced. She had a sheet of stars ready, so those who failed to make it in the top three did not go empty-handed.

Between herself and those expectant eyes, she'd arranged a table and covered it in straw. She'd dipped in her own pocket to buy a bag of the stuff from the local pet store. It looked great with the decorated eggs lined up. They were all hardboiled – at least she hoped, because if not, things could get messy. Some sat in painted egg cups or cartons, others simply cradled in straw or strips of paper, all of varying colours. Some were simple, others were impressive. One, thought Kelly, looked like the kid had scribbled over it with a permanent marker. There were of course superheroes and Pokemon just as she'd predicted. Parents had helped with a few, that was evident.

Her wooden egg lay on its side next to the stapler she kept at hand on her desk. Her coffee sat there getting cold. Perhaps she'd been too excited for this herself.

"They are all very, very good," she said.

So many wide eyes stared back.

"And," she added, "you know I can only pick three."

So many grins.

"This one is good." She picked up an egg that was painted black and had pointy ears. "Batman."

At the back of the class, a blond boy named Jeremy MacDonald clapped and the other children turned to look at him. "That's mine!" he shouted.

She nodded, knowing that it would be his. He always ran around the playground pretending to be Batman. Often, she'd have to tell him to be quiet in class because he'd be talking about a Batman comic or the Batman cartoon or the new Batman movie.

"This one is clever." She pointed to one that sat in a crushed egg cartoon that had been painted green and brown. The egg itself was painted grey, and pierced through the top of the shell was a small plastic cocktail stick shaped like a sword. She read the banner along the edge of the carton. "Eggscalibur."

Frizzy-haired Sarah Jenkins waved. "Daddy said that would win."

"Did he, now?" Kelly smiled and moved further along the table. "You all have made my job very difficult."

The children started to talk at once, the classroom becoming an uproar of excitement. She picked up several others in turn, moved them around in their nests, pointing and smiling, all the while the cacophony increased.

"Okay, okay," she eventually said, "quiet now, please."

All eyes shifted back to her and the eggs, and their voices quieted. Soon, most of them were silent. A few whispers lingered, but that was fine.

"Which of these will be the runner up?" she asked.

"Mine!" shouted Joey Frank; a pleasant kid, indeed, the class jester. Intelligent, if only he applied himself to the work given to him, rather than trying to be the centre of attention. "You gotta pick mine as the winner!"

As it was, Kelly had no idea which one could be his. Perhaps it was the octopus, or the Teenage Mutant Ninja Turtles. She really had no clue.

There was even an egg covered with cotton wool, shaped into a rabbit. She picked it up. One of the cardboard bunny feet hooked up a piece of straw. No way had a ten-year-old made this. Did the parents really think they'd pull the wool – or rabbit fur – over her eyes? She placed it back down and picked up one that had been painted with a steady hand. Nothing fancy, just circles and lines of dark blues and purples, reds and yellows. Very pretty. This certainly could've been painted by one of the more artistic kids.

"This is good," she said. "Perfect angles."

Bethany Simmonds, seated at the back in the far corner, smiled and lowered her eyes. Always a shy one. She'd get far in the creative arts should she pursue it, Kelly was certain. This wasn't the first time she'd thought such things of the girl's talent.

Kelly brushed her fingers over several others.

"I think—"

Something fell behind her, cracking as it hit the floor.

~

The wooden egg lay in pieces. A frothy, green-grey mess oozed between the splinters, sections of the intricate design floating as the mess spread. It ate into the floor, hissing. Tiny wisps of smoke curled upwards. Stepping back, Kelly's arse hit the table. She yelled. The kids began chatting animatedly, some getting out of their seats. But she didn't look at them, she only heard the clatter of chair legs, their frenzied voices. All she could do was watch as that bubbling goo spread and burnt into the floor.

"Get out!" she screamed. A putrid stink stung her nostrils. It was like rubber, vegetation, and something rotten. "Now!"

The stuff frothed and spat, peppering the front panel of her desk. From the spreading mass, thick tendrils of what looked like vines hooked out and shot across the floor. Tiny veins crackled along their lengths, splaying outward like a growing fungus. It looked like the creepers you'd find in a forest, only sentient, reaching, searching …

"Move!" she shouted at the class. She backed up, further away from her exit. "Get out!"

Amid scattered chairs and shunted tables, the children were funnelling towards the open door. Shouts echoed from the hallway.

More vines crept outward and Kelly backed up further, stamping and kicking at the creepers. One becoming five, becoming ten, becoming twenty, unfurling. She scrambled backwards, yelling. Her desk jolted, tilted into the sagging mass of creepers. Pencils and pens rolled first, then several notebooks slid forwards, everything sank into the nest – it *was* like a nest, for God's sake. This was insane.

Last to fall was the laptop and telephone.

She staggered further back, kicking at a thrashing vine.

The contest table jerked and shifted sideways. In a tangle of straw, all the children's eggs fell into the widening expanse of stitched vines. The centre of the nest deepened to become more a pit. The seething mass rustled and snapped as twigs and sticks wound around each other, reinforcing the whole damn thing. More vines branched out, shooting outward, clutching table legs. A thin veiny fungus coated everything like a kind of webbing.

Kelly had now backed up to the wall and shimmied around a cupboard. She had to get out of there. Most of the children had scrambled from the classroom, but some of the littler ones scuttled behind. Some slipped on the pens and pencils and rulers and books that littered the floor. Their cries echoed in the near empty room.

As Kelly rounded a number of upended desks and chairs, she kept glancing at the growing nest.

Bethany and Joey were the last children running towards the door.

A vine shot out and caught the girl's skinny leg. She crashed to the floor and shrieked. One shoe flew from her foot. Tiny creepers slithered around her ankle and dragged her back … towards the nest.

Joey scrambled for the door, but tripped over his classmate.

Kelly darted towards the pair of kids. Their screams filled her head. The room had darkened, the nest now expanding even further, swallowing tables and chairs. More vines slithered out, making wispy noises as they slid against the dry creepers that lined the nest. With her breath coming in gasps, she tasted foliage and vegetation.

A vine had now coiled around Joey's ankle, and both kids shouted, scrambling uselessly as they were dragged closer towards more eager vines.

"Joey!" Kelly leapt forward. On her knees, she grabbed the vine that clamped his leg. Its rough bark scratched her skin as she tore it free. "Run!"

The vine blindly slapped the floor.

He scrambled for the door and she watched him head for the hallway. Further away, Bethany flailed. Tears streamed down her red cheeks. Her hands raked the floor, now closer to the nest. The vines stitched around her legs, then her body vanished into the spreading nightmare.

"Bethany!" Kelly yelled.

Screams and shouts dwindled far out in the hallway, beyond the classroom.

Kelly wanted to get out, to run the hell away from this madness but—

What the hell was she doing?

—She leapt over a thrashing stumpy vine and launched herself towards the girl, arms outstretched. Her chest thumped the thatched vines and sticks. Her breath rushed from her lungs. As she gulped air, that stink poured down her throat. A miasma of light fizzed across her vision and soon the darkness closed in. She clambered through the tangle of scratchy vines, kicking and punching as they grabbed for her. She wriggled further into the nest.

Darker and darker.

She focused on Bethany's pale face, keeping the poor girl in sight as the nest dragged them both into its heart ...

~

Joey hugged himself as his mum drove him away from school, leaving behind so many blue flashing lights. He'd never before seen so many policemen and police cars. He didn't know if he should feel excited or scared. Again, he thought of Bethany and his teacher, Mrs Laurence.

He still felt as though the branch thing held his ankle.

His mum said to him, "Let's get some chips, shall we? We can eat them while we walk between the fisherman huts. You always enjoy looking at the boats."

He did. He liked the way they sat on the beach, out of the water. Sometimes he'd even seen the little yellow tractors pull them from the sea.

When his mum got to a red traffic light, she put her hand on his head. She always smelled of coconut. His head didn't hurt anymore from when he'd smacked it on the floor after tripping over Bethany. He wondered if she was still inside that giant bird's nest. Ever since managing to run away, all he thought of was how all those weird branches and sticks had swallowed Bethany. And Mrs Laurence. He liked Mrs Laurence. Bethany, too.

He hoped they were okay.

When the traffic light turned to green, his mum squeezed his neck a bit too tightly and let go. His ankle itched a bit. Nothing was there though, and the nice man from the ambulance had said he was okay.

The drive down to the seafront was no different than usual, and Joey squinted into the red lights of all the cars in the traffic. His mum had recently told him that the sky was darker because in winter the sun was further away, and now in spring, the sun was getting closer. He pictured the sun as a tiny yellow marble far away in space. Mrs Laurence had once explained that the Earth evolved – or was it revolved? – around the sun. It was dark in space. Like the middle of the nest had been, before it closed in on his friend and teacher, like dirty water rushing down a plughole. It had vanished. He remembered how some of the desks and chairs were broken, but the nest had gone. Like it had never even been there.

He was hungry.

Soon they walked across the car park, both with a bag of chips in hand. His mum had got a large bag for herself and him a small bag. Their portions looked the same size though. They ate them while walking between the fisherman huts where it always smelled of salt and grease, and of course fish.

Somewhere nearby, plastic rustled on the wind.

Beneath his shoes, pebbles and pieces of wood clicked and crunched. There was some string on the ground, too. They walked past chunks of white stuff that looked like lumps of snow. He knew it wasn't; it was actually broken bits of the packing that came in boxes to stop things from breaking. It was called 'polystylean' or something. There was always rubbish laying around there, but Joey always liked it. Further down, closer to the beach, he'd see some boats up on stilts. He liked that word: stilts.

The cold air numbed his fingers and he wanted to put his gloves on, but he knew he couldn't eat chips that way, he'd get tomato sauce on them. Seagulls circled overhead, some landed on the pebbles and hopped nearby. Several watched him from the flat roofs. Most likely they wanted one of his chips. He was glad he wore his woolly hat and scarf.

"Maybe afterwards we can go and get you a chocolate egg," his mum said to him.

That made Joey think of those eggs he and his friends had painted ... and the way Mrs Laurence's wooden egg had split open to spread the branches and sticks around the classroom.

And he again thought of how one had grabbed his ankle.

His mum walked further ahead of him. She passed a stack of red and white baskets that leaned against a hut with walls of peeling black paint. Usually there would be smelly fish in them, but these were filled with the worn and smooth planks he sometimes saw washed up on the beach. Green-black seaweed wrapped around them and draped down onto the dusty pebbles.

A fisherman stood in a doorway, his face hidden in the shadows of both the gloomy hut and his cap. He wore a long coat that reached down to his Wellington boots.

Joey saw the man's cap tilt as though he watched him approach. He dropped the chip he was about to eat.

The man also held something.

He stopped and stared while his mum kept walking, rounding the corner of the hut. His mouth went dry.

The man – was he a fisherman? – held an egg.

Joey heard his mum's shoes get fainter as she walked further away.

The egg that the man held was like the one Mrs Laurence had on her desk, the one that had cracked and all that horrid stuff had come out. It was almost the same; the top was still smooth, yet to be carved.

Suddenly Joey was no longer hungry.

Behind the man, a bird flew around inside the hut. But it was too dark to see what type of bird. He didn't think it was a seagull, it was too black and had a long straight beak.

Joey wanted to run yet he didn't dare.

The man stepped forward and gravel crunched beneath his wellies. His jaw moved behind his beard as though he said something, but Joey couldn't hear. In the man's other hand was a knife. It gleamed in the daylight.

Joey felt his stomach jump.

The man lifted the knife and began carving the egg. Tiny slivers of wood curled away and fell to the ground. He wasn't even watching what he was doing, instead he continued to stare at Joey, those tiny eyes squinting beneath bushy eyebrows.

"What is it, Joe-Joe?" His mum's voice drifted back to him, seeming far away.

Joey knew she stood somewhere nearby, but he didn't look at her. He watched the man raise the egg above his head.

She asked, "What's he doing?"

~

Kelly Laurence slid through the suffocating muck of slippery vines, further into the cloying darkness. It was as though she tumbled rather than being dragged, and by now, the creepers had become wetter, slimier. Still, her determination kept her pressing onwards. It was all she could do to keep upright, often slipping onto her chest. Her arms and shoulders and legs were killing her. She clambered through what was like the dense undergrowth of a forest floor, with tangled branches and brambles catching her now-drenched hair.

As for Bethany, Kelly could barely see the girl as those vines continued to drag her deeper into the nest. However, the surrounding creepers had long since receded enough to allow Kelly more leverage, more manoeuvrability.

How long had she been scrambling through this hell?

Her knees and feet slipped, and her hands grasped at the slick creepers. It reminded her of the time she'd fallen down a river bank and landed in the thick mud at the water's edge. Clumps of reeds had snatched her and the more she'd struggled, the more she sank, the water soaking her to the skin. Although that water had been cold, this insane place was warm, its atmosphere sweaty.

A rising fog had also started to curl from the glistening vines.

And the stink. It was incredible. Raw, meaty, like sewage. It clogged her nose, filled her throat, tasted like shit. Her teeth clenched so tight her jaw ached. How much longer could this go on?

She scrambled over a mound of splintered creepers. They were soft rather than sharp. For the umpteenth time, she cried, "Bethany!" and ended up coughing. That stench filled her lungs.

Why were those vines dragging the girl and not her? It was almost as though they were sentient, recognising that Kelly was in pursuit. Not only that, where were they taking her?

Kelly slid downwards, still scrambling after the girl, and twisted awkwardly to land on her arse. Water or filth or slime, whatever the hell it was, soaked straight through to her underwear. This was even warmer, hot in fact. Several creepers whipped her face and then recoiled. She swatted them away and she pushed herself sideways and sat up, hoping to not have lost sight of the girl.

"Bethany!"

Just ahead, the child hung suspended in the cross-hatch of thick vines and tangled creepers. These glowed purple, a strange luminescence in the gloom. They creaked as they tightened around her, squeezing. Her eyes were closed; she looked so peaceful, even though she was caked in black, glistening muck.

"Bethany!" Kelly yelled again and gulped the foul air. She choked.

As though relaxing, the vines released the girl and she fell. Her tiny – lifeless? dear God, no! – body slapped the ground. The black stuff splashed Kelly's face. She lurched forward, knee-deep in fog and filth. Bethany's eyes were closed but she breathed softly. Black bubbles dribbled over her lips.

Cradling the girl, Kelly gently slapped her cheek. "Bethany?"

Her eyes fluttered, opened, and widened. She screamed. Sharp and shrill. It was a flat echo.

"It's okay," Kelly whispered.

A rustling noise made her look up. Overhead, something shifted in the thatch of dripping creepers. Her heart pulsed in her throat, and she held her breath. What was it? She squinted. Nothing. Had something been there? She listened, yet heard nothing more.

Bethany mumbled and wriggled, and still Kelly looked up, her neck stretched. She felt as though she knelt on a forest floor, peering into a desperate twilight that leaked through dense branches. And somewhere in those branches … was that a pair of eyes reflecting the strange luminescence of fog and purple vines?

Her breath snatched her throat and she coughed.

The filth around her started to froth, more of those purple vines churning the muck and creating clouds of billowing fog.

Kelly and Bethany clutched one another. The girl sobbed and coughed and choked, her tiny arms and legs twitching. All the while the fog thickened. A bitter taste filled Kelly's mouth and she coughed again, great chest-rattling whoops.

More trunks thrashed in the muck, spraying them both. And the fog swirled and snaked around them, the darkness closing in …

Still Kelly felt those eyes watching them.

~

The fisherman hurled the egg across the yard and it smashed into the wall of another hut. Black and green filth spattered the brickwork. Immediately, sticks and twigs and branches shot out, whispering and rustling, snapping and cracking, splaying outward. It was another nest – exactly the same as Joey had seen in the classroom that morning – and it filled the area between him and his mum. It deepened as it spread.

The ground rumbled, and the pebbles tittered against one another.

"Joe-Joe!" his mum yelled. "Get back!"

Joey didn't realise he'd dropped his bag of chips. The paper shivered on the pebbles as the ground shook. He staggered away.

A fog drifted up from the middle of the nest.

Followed by a hand.

Black slime caked it, the fingernails like claws. Another hand reached out, then someone's head, again slick with that disgusting, gloopy mess. Fog clouded the sky and with it a nasty stink that was like rotten vegetables, and farts.

Joey watched as out came—

~

Kelly gulped fresh air. She smelled the sea, fish, and even grease. But thankfully no more tasting the cloying fog and shit of decay and vegetation from the hell she'd just endured. She pulled Bethany free from the clutches of the vines and their rough bark. The poor child had cried herself into twitchy robotic movements.

Together they emerged, dripping filth, and squinting into the daylight.

Where were they?

The vines and creepers settled as she clutched Bethany tight and clambered up and out of the nightmare. No longer were those vines trying to keep them in; it was as though they'd given up trying to imprison them.

Black walls and blue barrels, red and white crates and – how did they get here? They were all the way down by the sea, at the Fisherman's End. She'd expected to emerge back in her classroom, but why here?

Every one of her limbs screamed at her, her skin raw, her clothes saturated.

How long had she been in there, dragging both Bethany and herself through the embrace of slime and jungle-like foliage?

She coughed and spat. The stuff tasted foul.

Around her, the wood began to crumble, dust pluming, replacing the fog to drift upwards to an overcast sky. The ground levelled out, eventually flattening. No more vines, no more creepers, no more of that foul stink.

Everything was normal.

Apart from the taste.

She spat again.

Kelly then saw a woman crouch and take Bethany from her. For a moment, she was reluctant to release the girl … yet the woman smiled. She recognised her as one of the mums. Couldn't place a name, though. Behind her was Joey Frank. Of course, the woman was Mrs Frank.

Kelly coughed.

Joey stared at one of the huts. A fisherman stood watching them, although he had his head tilted as though speaking with someone behind him. He held a woodcrafter's knife. Something dark inside the hut shifted, something large.

The man stepped aside.

Mrs Frank said something, but Kelly didn't hear. The sound of the shrieking winged *creature* – it was most definitely not a bird – clawed its way around the door frame. The wood splintered beneath its talons.

Its eyes burned yellow in a head that was nothing more than a twisted mess of blistered flesh and fur. Its beak was as black as its charred flesh and as long as a bread knife. And just as serrated. Leathery wings slapped against its wrinkled body as the thing scrambled past its master. Extending great wings, it launched into the sky. Its cry drilled into Kelly's brain and she clamped hands to her ears. Mrs Frank and her son both did the same.

Bethany was hunched over, clutching her stomach. She coughed, choking, and spat green filth onto the pebbles.

The fisherman stepped aside, arms folded. He nodded and watched the winged demon – that was what it was, surely, considering the hell she'd just climbed through – circle above. Its impressive wingspan thumped on the air to create a wind that froze her wet scalp.

Kelly shivered and coughed, and agony spiked her stomach. She hugged herself. A dizziness swept over her, black and white flashes blinding her. The pain raged in her stomach, up into her chest.

Bethany was sobbing and coughing, and—

The little girl spat out a glistening egg as black as onyx. It clattered across the pebbles and rolled to a stop. The poor girl's eyes widened, and she staggered back, screaming.

A bitterness rose into Kelly's throat, and she heaved. Breathing sharp, hissing through the nose, she again coughed, wracking, thundering through her chest. Dear God, the pain ... and she buckled over. Her palms hit the uneven ground and she slipped, her nose inches from the ground.

Absolute agony tore up her throat ...

And she, too, spat out an egg.

Followed by vomit.

The stink clawed up her nostrils.

Overhead, the sound of those flapping wings got closer and that freezing wind strengthened.

Something thumped into Kelly's ribs and the air rushed from her lungs. She smacked into a blue barrel and it threatened to topple. It didn't.

The demon-bird-thing had both eggs clutched in its chipped talons and it rose higher, its shriek now an intermittent chirp. Like the damned thing was happy.

It had offspring, why wouldn't it be happy?

Kelly actually laughed at the insanity of it.

Mrs Frank had both Bethany and Joey in her arms, cradling them tight. The children sobbed. Tears glinted on the woman's cheeks, her eyes moist and wide.

Kelly watched the creature as it flew over the boats, out over the sea and towards the horizon, to become a black dot. Its sporadic cries echoed, dwindling the further it went. When she finally looked away, she noticed the fisherman was no longer there.

YOU HAVE ONE MESSAGE

Jonathan Broughton

The sun blazes in a cloudless sky and the calm blue sea sparkles. A perfect day, a heart-warming, spirit soaring day. I sit at my laptop and organise my tax returns. Not an exciting exercise, though necessary and the bright light helps, encouraging my fingers to glide across the keys. The numbers add up, or not, show more loss than profit, hint at lifestyle changes for saving money. These are to be ignored or implemented at some future date and the choices I make then will be dependent upon my mood. They have no place in today's brightness. Like lumpy shadows, they hide in dark corners and fester and, with luck, will be forgotten.

My mobile rings. The tune is famous, the rendition loose. The Queen of the Night's aria from Mozart's 'The Magic Flute.' I know who's calling, Samantha, to arrange the time of our lunch date.

"Hello?" The line clicks and pops. "Hello?" I check the screen. It is Samantha. "Hello?" A low buzz, another click and then, nothing. Dodgy reception? The line is still connected. I listen once more. Silence and I tap *Disconnect*. My battery metre reads full, my reception is at maximum, so the fault isn't mine.

Samantha's driving down from the City so I won't ring back. Knowing her, she's forgotten to bring her hands-free kit. She'll try again when she's closer.

Back to the accounts. I finish February, just March to go. Hurray! I stretch and enjoy the sun's warmth as it pours through my open window.

A skateboarder below me on the promenade weaves to a sudden halt and reaches into his jeans pocket. His mobile is touchscreen too, like mine, and he clamps it to his ear. I see his mouth moving, his frown, his glance at the screen, his repeated words. I think like me, he is saying "Hello?" He shakes the phone, listens again, gives up and, with sharp impatience, thrusts the phone back into his pocket.

Is he with the same provider? Is there a more general problem? I decide it is coincidence, though I angle my phone out of the sunlight so that the screen is shaded, just to check.

You have one missed call.

Odd. The phone didn't ring, didn't vibrate and beep to alert me to a new message. I tap *Show* and the screen flickers to Samantha's details. I tap *Return* and wait for the call to connect.

It clicks again and buzzes. Then patters, like fingernails on glass. The screen tells me it is connected.

"Samantha?" It whines and crackles. "Can you hear me?" Buzzes and hisses. "Samantha?" The hissing increases. I tap *Disconnect* and the screen goes blank, turns blue, fades into an island beach with palm trees. My default picture. Reception maximum, battery full and a new message.

You have one new Voicemail.

Ah! Is my phone on the blink? I haven't dropped it. I open the dialler and press *One*.

Connecting to Voicemail.

The automated voice speaks: "You have no new messages. To change mail box features ..." What? I press *Seven* for saved messages. Her message might have stored automatically. The line whirrs, buzzes, hisses. I disconnect and try again. There is no automated voice and the hissing is louder.

I toss the phone onto the pile of papers beside me. I check my watch, quarter to twelve. Samantha won't be here for another hour. I guess she will suggest we meet at one. It's just a question of where. Plenty of time to finish my accounts, but my mind won't focus. Has she had an accident? Is she trying to contact me with a damaged phone?

Ring her, make sure she is safe. I select her name, choose *Call* and press. And wait. There is no ring tone, yet something, voices, static, it is too faint to be discerned, rolls like distant waves just beyond hearing.

"Samantha?" Silence. Then my voice echoes back. "Samantha ... antha ... tha ... Samantha ... antha ... tha ..."

I am connected, the screen tells me so.

"Samantha ... antha ... tha ..." The echo doesn't diminish, but repeats like a stylus on a scratched vinyl.

I disconnect and drop the phone onto the papers. I peer, unfocused, at my laptop screen. Worry makes my stomach tingle. What's happened? Has anything happened? Is it just ... poor reception? Or is she tangled and bleeding in the middle of a pile of smoking metal?

I press my thumbs into the desk's sharp edge until they ache. Stupid, idle speculation. Concentrate, finish the accounts, it's just atmospherics, but first I need another cup of coffee.

BBC Radio Four, turned low, mumbles in the kitchen. No problems with the BBC then. The boiling kettle obliterates the voices and every other sound too. I choose instant, lazy, but quick.

Atmospherics? It might be. Residual particles left over from last week's solar flare? Yes, but that was last week. News bulletins warned of possible disruption to electrical supplies, because of the ferocity of the flare. And Saturday evening, the lights dipped three or four times. That was all, there were no blackouts, anywhere I don't think, in the world. Was the flare even bigger than they expected? I would have heard about it. A major news story like that.

I stir my coffee to a shade of dark brown and return to my desk.

My phone is vibrating. It shudders upon the papers, on and on and on. It has never done this before. When it vibrates, it beeps, sending out two short staccato bursts accompanied by an equal number of violent shakes. I pick it up and my fingers tingle. The screen is blank, my picture gone, my shortcuts too.

What the hell? Outside, a girl screams. She is surrounded by others her age, boys and girls. They all hold mobiles, stare at them, glance from one to another with open mouths and wide eyes that hint at fear. The girl who screamed, drops her phone. It hits the concrete, part of it breaks off, but I can see it still vibrating. It judders across the pavement towards the girl's feet and she jumps back, her hands to her face.

All along the promenade, people stop and stare, hands lifted, some at arms' length as if frightened of their phone's behaviour. Cars pull up at the side of the road, necks craning, as they peer, scrutinise, and wonder.

I hurry back to the kitchen and turn up the volume on the radio. It is a discussion about the weeks' business in Parliament. I go into the lounge and switch on the television. There is no interference, it appears normal. I flick through the channels to the rolling news. There is a sports report on the BBC, a feature on Mexican drug gangs on Sky. I hop between them both, waiting for them to return to the studio. When they do, I flip-flop, first to one, then the other, but there is no breaking news about solar flares, or interference disrupting mobile phones. I leave the television on, return to the radio. The same voices, the same discussion.

I approach my desk, the phone is silent and still. The default picture has returned and my shortcuts and – a new message.

You have software updates. Press Install or Remind Me Later.

I glance out of the window. The sun beats upon my face and I flush from its heat. All along the promenade, people, huddled in groups, confer. Cars are parked at haphazard angles, half-on and half-off the pavement. Other drivers take advantage of the empty road and zoom past.

I pick up my phone and press *Install.* A white line with a blue spiral appears along the bottom of the screen. The spiral rotates, like an old fashioned barber's sign outside a shop. This is normal. *Updating* flashes up. The spiral rotates. In a moment, it will disappear and be replaced by a solid blue line that fills in the white line. In a moment. The screen flickers, fades, returns and then snaps to black.

A murmur of voices from outside, the words are unclear, but their tone is one of exasperation, some of anger. I depress the top button on the phone to switch it off. Count to ten and press it again to turn it on. Nothing happens.

Now I am angry and drop the phone with deliberate abandon onto my desk, where it lands with a clatter. I snatch up the receiver to my landline. There is a dialling tone and I punch in Samantha's number. The dialling tone purrs on, oblivious to my instructions. I try again with the same result. I attempt to reach the operator, a three-digit combination that registers on the screen, but not on the line. I slam the receiver into its cradle. Then I check the wireless hub under the desk. None of the green lights, for the phone or the Internet, flicker. The wall plug is in, the switch on. Online surfing with the laptop is out.

What is happening? Anxiety and anger are a bad mix. The day has soured, though, I console myself, it has soured for everyone, at least, those that I can see outside my window. Is it general? Or just here? Where is Samantha?

The television presenters prattle on with professional poise. The breaking news banner repeats stories of bomb blasts in Afghanistan and the changing fortunes of the golfers at the Masters. Then, on Sky, it changes. There is an amazing scientific breakthrough in Switzerland. The Hadron Collider has succeeded in detecting the Higgs boson elementary particle. I wait for the presenters to report a more detailed account, but they cut to a debate about world business.

Parliament is still being discussed on the radio. Which is odd. This programme lasts half an hour. Its slot finished ten minutes ago. An extended edition? I concentrate on what is being said. The rise in the state pension is not in line with inflation, even with the added bonus of subsidised fuel bills, pensioners are still worse off than a year ago. Does this really warrant extra time?

Then my phone rings. Its high shrill tone makes me jump. I run back to my desk, but I do not pick it up. Through the open window comes a cacophony of discordant sound. Is every mobile along the promenade and in the cars, ringing? People's hands jab as they attempt to connect.

My screen flashes, Samantha. Fear flutters at the edges of my mind, but I pick up the phone. I press *Accept,* again and again and again. The phone rings and rings and will not respond to my repeated efforts.

Seagulls rise from the rooftops and flock with cries of alarm. An old lady collapses onto the pavement and covers her ears. A man hurls his mobile over the railings into the sea. The electronic blast of jarring harmonies might be the only sound on earth, for it is all there is, with the seagulls, circling, squawking, watching.

My instinct is to run, to join the crowds along the promenade, seek reassurance from my fellow men, but what can we do, what can any of us do, to alleviate anxiety when events are unknown and strange?

I leave the phone on my desk, back out of the study and into the lounge. The soothing voices of the news presenters offers some balm. Still no story about the Hadron Collider, though it scrolls along the Breaking News banner.

Even now, I can hear the phones in the flats around me. Running footsteps pummel past my door, a baby cries and a dog barks, high-pitched and terrified.

Then I see it. The merest flick or click on the television screen. As if a tape has been refreshed by *Repeat*. The banner snaps off and then on. The presenters relay the news and after a minute, as if they are set to *Automatic*, they tell it again. And again.

I stumble into the kitchen. I am sweating, terror builds like a flood inside me. On the radio, details about the state pension are analysed and, a minute later, analysed again. I hit the *Off* button, but the voices chatter on. I yank the plug from the socket. Still the voices chatter. I turn the volume to low, but it does not diminish.

Then, silence. Not from the radio or the television. The phones have stopped ringing. The relief, so unexpected, makes me gasp and I stride back to the study.

The mobile's screen is blank and black. Is it on, or off? I pick it up. My greasy fingers leave smear marks across its black shining surface.

I open my desk drawer, rummage through its untidy mess and find the phone's charger. I attach it, plug it in and switch it on. There is no response. I press the *on/off* button, with no result. I press all the external buttons. Fear makes me angry as each button is pressed harder than the time before. The bastard thing!

Furious, I disconnect the charger and tug the plug from the socket. My T-shirt is soaking with sweat. What am I supposed to do when nothing works? Who can I tell when I can't communicate? What in pity's sake is going on?

Impotent, my mind blanks, my body stiffens into inactivity and I slump into my chair. The day is so hot. Sweat drops drip over my keyboard and sink between the gaps. Outside, people raise their phones above their heads and circle, first one way and then the other, as they attempt to track a signal. It looks weird, like a ritual, or a salute. One man even clambers up onto his car roof.

Is Samantha scared? Is she alone? I think she will look for help. She is outgoing, fearless sometimes, not afraid to talk to strangers. Concern and an instinctive desire to co-operate in a crisis, will draw her to others as they attempt to understand. I miss her, I want to talk to her, to soothe and reassure us both, but what can I do?

There is an odd silence, like an indrawn breath, an expectant hush. Even the seagulls, though still airborne, circle in soundless sweeps.

The phone shudders, stops. The screen flickers and the picture materialises. Raised voices carry through the window. There are no new messages, no prompts for updates. I cannot touch the phone, only watch, as if waiting for something to happen.

A high-pitched buzzing, which at first I take to be a mosquito, thickens to a deeper tone, and builds. Static, that crackles and hisses, whispers from the phone. I clench my teeth. With a sudden jump, the volume increases. I leap from my chair to the end of the desk. White noise, insistent, maddening and increasing. The sound amplified by every phone inside the flats and out. It soars to a sharper screech. I reel back and clamp my hands over my ears.

There is no respite. My body jolts in shock. Light and sound clash. Louder still and louder.

"Help!" I cry. Who can hear? People collapse on the promenade, writhe in agony, hurl their phones as far as they can throw them. My head is splitting, my eardrums burst, blood trickles through my fingers and down my arms.

A strident voice shrieks behind the static. Unheard-of words scream, piercing like broken glass that slices flesh.

I fall to my knees, my face to the light. The air shimmers with heat and the sun blazes.

THE COMMISSION

Mark Cassell

I jam on the footbrake as steam rushes against the windscreen. Like heavy fog it obscures my view of the road, swallowing the night. The engine dies and the headlights blink out, snatching a silence and deep blue darkness around me. Without streetlights for guidance, I coast the camper van over the white line I no longer see. Power cut *and* the radiator blowing? Not good. I'm not a mechanically-minded guy, and this is bad timing.

I crank up the handbrake. A couple of key twists and everything remains dead. No lights, no power. I open the door and cold air rushes in. Gravel crunches as I step into the night and my face dampens, warmed in conflict with the November air. Steam churns and reaches up to a moon that hides behind dark clouds.

So close to my destination.

Typically, I haven't renewed my roadside rescue membership. Can't afford it. At least not until last week when I received an advance for tonight's midnight assignment to photograph a castle in the middle of nowhere. Once the photographs are in the hands of my client – a suited gentleman who'd insisted I call him Oscar – I would receive a final chunk of payment.

Steam coils from beneath the bonnet like smoke from between metal lips. Whatever the problem is, it's bigger than a dead battery. I'm not going to bother raising the bonnet because in truth, I'd not know what to look for.

Times like this, I craved a cigarette. Six months since giving up, and I'm not going to give in. Besides, it's a long walk back to civilisation, the Domesday town of Rye, and I'm actually closer to my destination than the town. Plus, I drive a camper so at least I have somewhere to sleep; I'd walk to town in the morning and... what, buy cigarettes? No, damn it, I'd find a local mechanic. Get it fixed for the drive back to London.

My eyes are gradually adjusting to the near-dark and I squint over the roadside fence, into the sprawl of fields. Somewhere nearby is Camber Castle. I scan the darkness.

There it is.

Its walled ruins squat on flat fields, little more than a silhouette perhaps half a mile from where I stand. Fate may have struck the van dead, but at least my subject is pretty close. Could be much worse. Last I'd checked, it was nine o'clock. Perhaps it's now around quarter past, and so gives me enough time to put my feet up before the hike.

I get back into the van and close out the cold. Pleased to have my woolly hat, I tug it snug over my head and hug myself. I have ages until I need to be at the castle. Last week when we'd met in London, my client had been most specific.

"Each photograph," Oscar said over the clatter of cutlery from an out-of-sight kitchen, "must, without fail, be taken between the hours of three and four in the morning."

The man who'd sat before me filled the opposite seat of the booth. He was tall as well as wide, and even his forehead was large. Grey hair shone beneath the overhead lamp. When we'd shaken hands, mine was almost crushed by his massive ones. Impressive for a man who had only two fingers and a thumb on one hand – I must admit it felt a little strange when our hands clasped. In addition, never before had I a client with such peculiar requests.

"The castle will feature in the first chapter of my next book," Oscar said. Those two fingers curled around the tea cup like a claw. "It has great historic significance to the theme."

"Theme?" I still grasped my mobile phone having just watched £1k appear in my bank account. "Tell me more."

"Secret histories in the British Isles."

"Is that why you want me there at that precise time?"

He sipped his tea. His eyes over the rim gave away nothing.

"Also," he added, "it is poignant to feature in the first chapter as I once lived in Rye. When I was a boy."

"What's so specific about Camber Castle?"

"Mike," he said, gulping the last of his tea, "you will have to wait until the book comes out."

I liked to think I'd get a courtesy copy, but I didn't voice this. Behind Oscar more patrons came in from the London streets, each shaking rain from coats and umbrellas.

"How many other places will be featured in your book?" I asked.

"A dozen, certainly. I suspect several more will come about as I immerse myself in research surrounding those already pinned."

I wondered if he'd commissioned other photographers from around the UK. Perhaps if he liked my work with this first castle, he'd take me on board. Hell, I could do with the money.

"I will meet you in Rye, Monday afternoon, and you will give me the memory stick. I've booked a room at a Bed and Breakfast there," he concluded.

"No problem."

We shook hands again and he got up to leave. Shrugging himself into his overcoat, he walked off and stopped at the door. He looked over his shoulder, his eyes piercing. "Remember, Bill. Sorry, remember Mike," he said across the heads of several coffee drinkers, "between three and four in the morning."

He pulled open the door. The rasping wet sound of tyres over tarmac, of engines and city life, drowned his footfalls into the grey day.

~

A metallic screech tears me from sleep. I jerk awake, my knee smacking the steering wheel. I stretch and pull myself upright, squinting through the windscreen. What is it? Where am I?

Broken down and waiting to photograph a castle, that's where. I blink.

Again, that sound.

It shrieks like something scratching the camper's bodywork. An animal? I fumble open the door and lurch into the night, my heart like thunder. Cold air chills my ears and pushes down my throat. A pale moonlight casts a shimmering glow across the tarmac and over surrounding hedgerows.

"Hey!" I shout. My voice bounces back in a flat echo.

I jog to the rear – no one – and press a palm to the cold paintwork. Something had dented the panel – no, it is more than a dent, it's a gouge about the same width as my hand. Difficult to see in the poor light, I crouch and look beneath the camper. Nothing but darkness. I run back to the driver's door and rummage in the side pocket to grab a torch. The beam spears the night and lights up the hedgerows. Nothing moves. It's silent too, save for the sound of my heartbeat. A quick scan beneath the camper again and the torchlight reveals nothing. Straightening up, I run a finger along the jagged edge of the damaged metal.

"What ...?" my breath plumes. I picture my bank account dropping a zero.

It looks as if the bodywork had been parted with a can-opener.

Something shrieks. Far away this time. Whether a bird or some other night creature, I've no idea. I peer along the bushes and ... What is that? A cluster of shadows moves. My stomach twists and I glance to my left, then to my right. Just the wind. Only the wind. This is absurd. I feel like a kid afraid of the dark.

I head back to the camper and I look at my watch: 3:35 a.m.

"Shit," I whisper.

There's nothing I can do about the damage. I have a job to do and I'm late. Still I can't think of any reason for Oscar to give me such a precise time, but I think of myself as someone good to my word; if I'm getting paid, I'll do everything to the letter.

Except for this morning, it seems.

After a rummage for my camera bag, tripod, and an LED panel, I'm outside again. With the camper locked up behind me, I follow my torch beam through bushes and into a field – the *first* field as I soon learn. I trudge across the flat grassland, coming to one gate and then another; each spring-loaded lock freezing to the touch and shrieking as I open it. That sound is a constant reminder of my damaged camper. A slight saltiness hugs the cold air, making me think of the seaside and wondering when I'd last visited the coast – most of my freelance photography is city-based. Dark clumps of what I assume to be sheep droppings litter the ground, and mud splashes onto my trousers and cakes my boots. A few times I have to circle marshy areas. I eventually keep parallel with the snaking darkness of a stream. All the while in the distance, Camber Castle draws nearer, squatting on the landscape with hunched shoulders.

Eventually I stand beneath the towering north wall, a rounded stretch of pitted and jagged sandstone the height of a two-storey building. Grass has sprouted from the walls, and moss like mustard thumbprints covers most of its surface. My torch spotlights chunks of ill-fitting rock and sometimes even brick; not the neatest of efforts in way of repairs. Near the top, askew from the barred and padlocked entrance, two gaping holes that I guess once housed heavy artillery reveals only the thickening clouds above. Still the moon is reluctant to guide my footing and several times the uneven ground, filled with grass tufts and pebbles, threatens to twist an ankle. The sheep droppings are worse here but it doesn't stop me from shouldering my bag to the ground.

I wander around the curving wall, impressed by the castle's overall girth. From what my two minute internet search had brought up, this 16th-century castle is little more than an octagonal fort sporting four D-shaped platforms and a gatehouse. As a coastal defence – back then the sea was a mile or so closer inland – this 'device fort' held a small garrison, yet never once saw action.

A sign exclaims: *DANGER. Climbing is forbidden on these walls as serious injury may occur.*

I drag a hand across the rough sandstone and it crumbles into powder. I certainly have no desire to climb.

A glance at my watch tells me it's almost four o'clock.

Returning to my bag I swiftly assemble the equipment. I set the tripod a fair distance away and aim the LED panel at a bastion to create a few sinister shadows. Oscar is, after all, writing about secret histories and what better way to suggest secrecy than by playing with shadows? By the time I would begin taking photos, the EXIF data would give away my late arrival. No matter though, as I can falsify it before handing Oscar the memory stick. I know the man had insisted that the photos are to be taken between three and four in the morning, but surely it can't be that important.

During the following half hour I circle the castle, resetting the tripod and angling the LEDs. My subject proves to be somewhat photogenic in its own ruined way, creating suitably majestic and eerie poses. The side facing the coast is the most damaged; proof of a relentless attack from over four centuries of wind and salt. One bastion in particular is pitted and holed like cheese.

That same wind howls in my ears.

By the time I make it back round to where I'd started, thankful to be out of the wind, I note I'd taken almost a hundred photos. The last few were aided by subtle moonlight.

One final time I set the tripod down and angle the LEDs. I go to switch on the panel, and—

Through a jagged hole in the outer wall secured with a metal grill, I see something shimmer in the moonlit shadows. Beyond those bars and deep within the castle itself, something moves, flitting between a pair of low walls surrounding a grass mound. A haze of mist drifts between tufts, curling and unravelling like fabric.

An icy touch crawls up my spine.

Nothing moves.

It must've only been the moonlight playing with the dense shadows or the fog unfolding inside the castle.

I take more photos before I detach the camera, and leaving the LEDs turned on I walk towards the grill. My silhouette dances up the sandstone wall, stretched limbs gangly and awkward, the silence of the night interrupted only by my heartbeat. The camera feels heavy, and my footfalls – surely too many for such a short walk – drag. I press my free hand against the gritty sandstone, the smell of it is strong. And something else ... something heavy and earthy. Beyond the grill the fog thickens.

The movement happens again, a shifting of white and grey.

Whatever it is had teased the fog into miniature whirlwinds that even now drifts into the fading moonlight.

Again silence descends.

I glance over a shoulder, not really knowing what to look for. I turn, stepping away from the wall, taking another step ... and then another.

Agony flares up the back of my neck, into my head.

Darkness claims me, only for a second. Lightning shards lance my vision, and my feet come off the ground. I'd tripped over something. My shout, stunted in a tight throat, echoes, muted by fog that tastes like earth, like the sea, like something dead. The ground rushes at me and my knees jar. I slide in the cold, soft mud. In front of me, in a swirl of dizziness, I see my SLR. I'd dropped it. Wisps of fog devour the strap and curl around the casing, teasing the lens.

Light dances in my eyes again like a dozen camera flashes.

Then there is only darkness.

~

The bleating of sheep tugs me awake.

I'm on my back. Clouds skid overhead on a crisp wind that cools my face beneath a dawn sunshine unusually warm for November. Blurred vision, sunlight, the stink of animals, wet clothes, mud. My vision sharpens and I see several of the sheep I'd heard. Their wool is tangled and clumped, and their breath plumes as much as my own. The nearest tilts its head at me then shuffles away.

I press palms to either side of my thumping head. Then I remember. Something had hit me and I'd tripped over.

Pushing my hands to the ground I prop myself up. My legs feel miles away as I drag them inward. I scratch the back of my head and my hand comes away sticky, fingertips glistening red. A wave of nausea crashes down and my vision blurs and refocuses. It's like I'm hungover.

I look behind me, up at the castle. The sandstone wall looms over me with an almost accusatory glare as though the artillery holes are eyes. Perhaps a part of the bastion had fallen on me. However, scanning the ground there's no evidence of this, and if that was the case then it couldn't have been that large as surely I'd now be dead.

With my head swimming I slowly stand, then stagger towards—

From a dry throat, I shout, "No!"

The tripod lay in three pieces, each leg buckled. The LED panel is cracked, wire protruding from smashed casing like spaghetti. All my equipment smashed, my bag shredded; thousands of pounds' worth now useless and scattered across the grass.

The sheep? Absurd. There's no way those animals could've done this. Some*one* had smacked me over the head, smashed my equipment, and done a runner.

"Bastards."

I drop to my knees besides my busted SLR. Again, dizziness sweeps over me. I fumble the muddy pieces. Ruined. I shuffle over to a tripod leg and grab it, brandishing it like a weapon. Breath short, I begin circling the castle. My head thumps as I stumble over uneven ground. No one is around, only sheep. I return to my ruined equipment overshadowed by a ruined castle.

At least I have my phone. I snatch it from my pocket (almost eight in the morning) and call Oscar. He answers after three rings.

"Good morning, M—"

"Someone's smashed my camera equipment."

Pause.

"Oscar, you there?"

"Where are you?" The man's voice is soft.

"At the castle."

"Are you okay?"

"My camera's ruined. I'm heading back to my van."

"Did you park—"

"Along the main road. I broke down and something tore a hole in the bodywork."

"I'll be there in fifteen minutes," he says and the line goes dead.

~

Oscar stares at the torn bag between me and the camper van, then leans back against his rental Ford Mondeo. It's silver and the diesel sticker on the fuel flap is curled at the edges.

A white van rushes past and then a motorcycle overtakes it, both heading towards Rye town.

I snatch brambles from my muddy jacket. I'd just this moment scrambled through the bushes, pretty much throwing my equipment on the ground. My trousers cling to my legs and my feet are freezing, socks wet. I'd returned in a straight line caring little for the swampy areas.

"We need to talk," Oscar says.

"You're not kidding." I step over the busted tripod and yank open the camper's passenger door.

Oscar scratches his jaw. "What time did you get there?"

I grab the tripod. "That's besides the—"

"No, it's not."

"What happened back there?" I throw the tripod into the footwell and return to the bag. My knuckles whiten as I grip the torn fabric and look up at him.

"I will pay for all these damages," he says, glancing towards the castle.

"Insurance will cover it."

"I will pay."

"Still not the point."

He nods.

I haul the bag into my arms and walk round to the open door. The return hike across the fields had taken twice as long, and I still feel like I'd necked a dozen pints. Lugging the split bag, traipsing across uneven fields and opening several gates hadn't made it easy. Oscar had parked in front of the camper awaiting my arrival. At least he'd helped carry my stuff through the bushes and onto the roadside.

Now, I glance at my client as I drop the bag onto the seat. I lean behind and rummage for some clean clothes and a pair of trainers. I change – it's bloody cold doing it at the roadside – and throw the whole muddy lot into the footwell. I slam the door. A truck thunders by, wind and dirt swirling.

"Okay," I breathe out, "talk."

The Ford's passenger door is open, pushed against the bushes. "Get in," Oscar says and walks round to the driver's side. He presses himself against the car as another truck shoots past.

I lock my van and head to the car, kicking a stone. It skitters across the tarmac to tumble into a pothole.

"Mike?" Oscar, now half in, half out of the driver's seat, looks at me over the car roof.

Giving my camper a final glance, scowling at the damaged wing, I slide into the car seat. We both close the doors at the same time. Mine is louder. It's an effort to pull the seat belt across and fasten it. The smell of coffee smothers me as does the soft interior.

Oscar starts the engine. "Do you need anything?"

"Just a cup of caffeine." I knock my head back and close my eyes as Oscar turns the car around. We head into Rye.

Eventually Oscar says, "You know I'm researching a book on places of interest."

"Yeah."

"Covering in particular, secret histories."

I open one eye and then the other. The day is turning into a bright one and does nothing for my thumping head. "Yeah."

"I'm specifically writing about places that are unknowingly haunted."

Out the window the road flies by. Fields, houses; a normal world.

"Are you telling me," I say, "that a ghost knocked me out and smashed up my equipment?"

Oscar's lips tighten.

"And the same ghost," I add, "punched a hole in the side of my camper?"

Still the other man says nothing.

"What do you take me for?"

"Someone," Oscar replies as he slows on approach to a pedestrian crossing, "who has fallen victim to the unexplained."

We creep to a halt as Oscar gives way to a man wearing a long overcoat. He doffs his hat at Oscar. I'm not certain but I think it could be a trilby – very old fashioned. If I wasn't so wound up, I probably would comment. Flashing images tumble across my vision and I squeeze my eyelids closed again. The torn panel of my van ... the flitting shadows in the castle ... the unravelling fog ... the whack across my neck ... my smashed equipment.

"Really?" The roiling collage of my insane Monday morning vanishes into the darkness behind my eyelids.

"Yes," Oscar says, simply.

"You could've warned me about the ghost." I open my eyes. "What's the deal? Not that I believe any of this, but talk to me. What's the story?"

He slows the car and pulls into a junction between black shiplap buildings typical of any harbour town.

"And," I add, "give me the shortened version."

"King Henry VIII," Oscar says, "sanctioned the construction of Camber Castle in the mid-16th century not to defend against possible French and Spanish invasion as historians claim, but to conceal something precious."

"Okay ..."

Already there are a number of people wandering the pavements, some even in the road. A mother pulls her son from the curb, closer to a shop display of pastel-coloured novelties.

"A powerful spirit with a unique power," Oscar continues, "is contained within the walls."

"Many places are supposedly haunted," I tell him, shaking my head.

Oscar steers the car past a restaurant-cum-coffee shop, and drives over white arrows and into a car park.

"Why did you want me to photograph the castle at stupid-o'clock?"

"Because," Oscar glances at me, "it was supposed to protect you."

"What the hell does that mean?"

"The time between three and four a.m. is known as the 'Dead Hour.'"

"Something with a name like that is supposed to protect me? This is bullshit."

He palm-steers the Ford into an empty space. "I assume you were late."

I glare at my client – my *client*, I must remember that. I'm here because I'm getting paid.

"That's all I've learned of this spirit." He cuts the engine and scratches his chin, fingernails scraping stubble.

We both watch the proprietor of a shop, its entrance flanked with old barrels and apple boxes, open the door to his first customer of the day. Suddenly I long for London, the buzz of life, carbon monoxide, looming grey buildings with sheet glass fronts, and people in business suits rushing around. Somewhere lacking castle ruins. A sign on black shiplap boards tells me this place is called the Strand. Hilarious, given that Rye is far removed from the Strand in London. When I emerge from the car I swear I can still smell sheep, swamp, and that fog. I rub my forehead. Had I really seen the shifting darkness inside the castle?

"Get yourself a drink," Oscar tells me from across the car roof, "I'll wait here."

Five minutes later, I cradle a coffee. With fingers curled around the cardboard, the heat barely penetrates my skin. For so late in the year this quaint harbour town seems busy. Several people are taking photographs of the buildings and the red telephone box across the way. I return to the car park; almost all the bays are filled. Oscar still stands beside his car watching a young family walk past. A boy of about six holds a plastic sword, swishing it back and forth. As I join Oscar, a rusty white van rounds the corner and chugs into the car park, heading for one of the last empty bays.

"Mike," Oscar says, "if you'd like to freshen up, come back to my B&B."

I poke fingers beneath my hat, scratching my scalp – I could do with at least washing my hands.

"Thanks."

We head across the road towards an incline where tarmac becomes cobbles green with moss. The pavement isn't wide enough so we walk in the road – it feels like I'm on a beach with stubborn pebbles— and as it steepens, a smell of soot strengthens with the wind. Late medieval and Tudor style houses hem us in where black cantilever beams project from white rendered walls. Ivy smothers some, and the twisting branches of naked wisteria frame a number of crooked windows. Between columns and pillars, oaken doors sit in wonky frames over uneven steps. Lanterns and actual door *bells* hang from rusted hooks. Oscar pauses once to scrutinise a door-knocker. It's a classic lion's head oxidised green by years of weather abuse.

"Bill lived at this house." His voice is strangely muted and I step closer. "Our mothers were friends and so were we. Thick as thieves."

I recall him mentioning he'd spent his childhood in this town.

He nods as though I'd spoken. "I failed him."

"What happened?"

"We were always adventurous boys, and we climbed over the castle wall. He was above me and the stone broke away. He fell. I managed to leap clear." He lifts his hand, staring at where the fingers once were. "But a stone crushed my hand. The rest of the wall landed on Bill."

I don't know what to say, and settle on, "Oh my God."

"They never found his head."

My throat felt as dry as the sandstone walls he speaks of.

"I often wonder what sort of man he would be today." Oscar straightens his back and his face hardens. "I will see him again, I am certain."

I have nothing to say; I hadn't labelled this man as religious, a believer of resurrection. But I guess losing someone at a young age in such an awful way must do *something* to you.

He walks off, head lowered, and I follow. By the time the road levels and we tread other streets, the sun gives in to an overcast sky. On the roof of the town hall, a flagpole sporting the Union Jack flaps in the wind. It sounds like someone repeatedly beating a pillow with a cricket bat.

I chew on my thoughts, as silent as Oscar. I want to ask more about the spirit, about the castle, and about Bill, but I don't.

A gentle mist tugs at every street corner, seeming to play with doorways, lampposts, and curbs. Eventually, we stand before a red door flanked by crooked bay windows. Behind the glass is a sun-bleached sign reading "B&B". Oscar pulls out a key and slips it into a lock surrounded by peeled paint. Before he turns it, the sound of something scraping against the cobbles makes us look back.

Across the street, teasing the rotten frame of a cellar door, the mist approaches. So similar to what I'd witnessed earlier at the castle. Mist doesn't scrape – it makes no sense – and I have no idea what made the sound.

Oscar is now inside.

I can't shake the thought of the mist, that *creeping* fog. It's as though it has a mind of its own. With a final glance backwards, I close the door behind me, thankful to be away from that peculiar stink now replaced by bacon and eggs. Clattering cutlery from the kitchen suggests where the owner is. Oscar shoots a curious look over his shoulder, his mouth downturned and eyes hollow. I follow him as he makes his way upstairs. Hideous wallpaper surrounds us; immense red flowers, faded and blooming over putrid yellow and green vines.

Perhaps I'm concussed, imagining things, but even looking at the wallpaper unnerves me.

We walk along a hallway and finally Oscar unlocks a door. We enter a room that parallels the decor of the rest of the Bed and Breakfast; sparse furniture between more disgusting wallpaper of age-bleached patterns. A suitcase is pushed in the corner with its innards bursting, which surprises me as I took Oscar to be neat and tidy in nature. The dresser, the mirror fastened in an ornate frame revealing a darkened reflection of the room, is cluttered with paper and something else I can't quite make out.

"Are they bones?" I ask as I get nearer.

Oscar doesn't answer.

I don't really want to know yet I have to ask, "Who do they belong to?"

Twenty-four hours ago, I wouldn't have guessed I'd be asking about bones while seriously considering the existence of ghosts. In light of what I'd so far experienced, today is turning me into a believer.

"Mine," he says and lifts up his right hand, wiggling the two remaining fingers.

We stand in silence for several seconds and eventually I go into the bathroom. Lavender overwhelms me. My hands curl around the edge of the cold basin as I stare into the mirror. My hat sits on my head askew and I straighten it. I look hungry and tired.

There's blood on my neck and I stagger back in panic.

My hand jerks to my throat and my fingers come away dry. No blood. I look back at my reflection. Nothing there.

"Tired," I tell myself and kick the door closed behind me, heart still pounding. After relieving myself, replaying in my head the entire morning's insanity, I scrub my hands while staring at my pale reflection. There's still no trace of blood; I must have imagined it.

I open the door and join Oscar. He sits on the edge of the bed, elbows on his knees, looking at the floor. He holds a large book, unopened, its cover browned and cracked with age. From this distance I can't read the title, but it looks like a bible.

"You okay?" I ask.

"There's something else." He looks up and scratches his cheek with those two fingers. "Something I need to get off my chest."

"What is it?" I wonder if things could get any crazier.

He places the book on the dresser.

Something scratches the window. We both twist round. Fog pushes against the pane, nothing more.

A coldness runs from my scalp, down my spine. "Oscar …"

He doesn't answer.

Is he smiling at me?

"We should go," I tell him. "It's the middle of the day, the fog…"

I cannot read his face. It's impassive.

"There's something about that fog," I say.

I stand and glimpse the book's front cover: *RESURRECTION FROM BENEATH*. I want to ask more about it but instead head for the door, Oscar close behind. What had he wanted to tell me? The handle is cold, like ice, and I tug it open.

Something shrieks again. This time out in the hallway. A metallic sound reminding me of my damaged camper. I don't want to, but I peer around the doorframe. Moisture dampens my face, and that all-too-familiar reek of fog slides down my throat. I wince. The one window that stretches along the hallway reveals a shrinking daylight, darkening to a premature dusk. Somehow the fog creeps inside the building, drifting along the hallway, tracing the edge of the rug and teasing the skirting. With it that damp smell, tinged with salt and vegetation.

My head whips back painfully as I'm shoved into the hallway. I smack the wall. Stunned, I spin round to glare at Oscar. His body seems to fill the entire doorway.

"What the hell?" I demand.

In his two-fingered hand, he cups the bones that had been on the dresser. His other hand clamps the doorframe, knuckles whitening.

I feel my cheeks warm. I press myself against the wall with nowhere to run – I'm at the end of the hallway. I'm not even near enough to a window to climb out. I would rather break a leg than step through the seething fog that now creeps towards us.

I can't tell what is louder, Oscar's breathing or my heartbeat.

"What's going on?"

A coldness grips my stomach.

His teeth clench, eyes darting from me to the top of the stairs, and then back to me. Around him, around us, the fog thickens, seeming to push away the ceiling, the hallway, the carpet. Moisture chills my face and with it comes a waft of that earthy stench.

I must get out of here. Now.

My perception shifts somehow. I can't quite make it out. Beside Oscar, the patterned wallpaper blisters. It peels away from him, neat and clean as though an invisible blade slices it. The mist toys with the unfurling edges and the paper parts horizontally, curling away from him. It curves slightly up and then down, heading towards the other end of the hallway. The other two doors shudder as the wood splits. Plaster crumbles and more wallpaper peels.

Still that fog thickens. Above the landing, a darkness tangles with the fog and a strange greyness shifts in the shadows that cling to the ceiling. Familiar. I've seen this before at the castle, and outside my camper.

"If only you had got to the castle at the time I told you."

"What?"

"None of this would now be happening," he says, "if you got there when I said."

I glance at the clogged shadows and spreading fog. A grey haze shivers, churns with the darkness, incorporeal at first to become a silhouette of—

"He's here!" Oscar shouts.

I don't know if he means me or the phantom, our nameless spirit that now seethes in the roiling fog. The silhouette sharpens, becoming a torso and stretched limbs. And something else … Something glinting, sharp.

Oscar steps from the doorway and approaches the spirit.

"Get back!" I yell. No matter the reason for his pushing me, I can't let him get nearer to that thing. My feet are rooted like I'm paralysed.

"I did everything I was supposed to," Oscar says, looking up into the swirling fog and shadow. "You promised that Bill would come back."

Does he believe his childhood friend is going to somehow be resurrected?

"You're mad," I tell him.

Without looking back, he points at me. "You should have taken him this morning."

My head knocks down a picture frame I didn't know was on the wall behind me. It smashes.

Again, there's the glint of something sharp in the overhead darkness.

Still Oscar approaches it.

"Take him!" he shouts. "Take him, now!"

The spirit shifts left and then right, a sharpening of shadow. Something long, slender, and catches a light that isn't there. Metallic. It sweeps up and down – a blade gripped in pale, claw-like fingers – and slants sideways.

The phantom blade slices through Oscar's neck in a dark spray. His head thumps onto the carpet, bounces and rests against the skirting. Fog swirls around those dead eyes, almost caressing his blood-peppered cheeks. Blood pools, creeping towards me like the mist, soaking into the carpet.

Chills claw up and down my back, numbing my toes, my fingertips, and freezing my scalp.

Oscar's headless body slumps to the floor; a soft sound, muffled by the churning fog. The blade, the phantom, shrinks into the shadows. The fog, too, recedes and as it does, it tugs at Oscar's clothes, at his arms, his legs, and severed head …

My spine hurts from where I press it against the wall, my entire body shivering as sunlight pours into the hallway. The air freshens as the final wisps of fog vanish with Oscar's body. The phantom, now gone.

And Oscar's head, no longer there.

All that remains, scattered across the carpet near my feet, are his finger bones. Pale, spotlighted by a sunshine that fails to warm me.

NORMAL, CONSIDERING THE WEATHER

Rayne Hall

18 May

Dear Gran,

How are things in Scotland? Here in Sussex, spring has finally arrived after weeks of grey mood-dragging drizzle – just in time for my annual leave. I celebrate the weather with a cream tea outside a traditional teashop on the beach.

They serve tea in flowery teapots, and the cup is one of those delicate porcelain ones with roses, gold rim and matching saucer. It's heavenly. Fat scones, slathered with strawberry jam and thick clotted cream, and I won't even think about the calories. I'll simply enjoy every bite.

My colleagues think it's silly that I should stay home for my annual leave, but I've never really visited the museum and the castle and play mini-golf, and it'll be fun to do all the touristy things. I wish you were here, and we could ride the rollercoaster together like we did when I was a kid.

When I finally unpacked my summer dresses last week, I wasn't sure if it would be warm enough – but it sure is! It feels so good to let the salt air and sunshine touch the skin on my arms. I may even get a tan. If this weather lasts, I'll spend my annual leave sunbathing on Hastings beach, with a bikini, a towel and a paperback.

The only nuisance is the many small black flies. I thought there must be a nest, but the waitress says the flies are everywhere today because insects due to hatch in April didn't get their cues, so when it finally grew warm, they all hatched in a single day. I pick them out of the clotted cream and use the spoon to save them from drowning in my tea; not nice at all.

Tomorrow, I'll come here and pen the next of my daily letters to you – handwritten on paper, the way you like them. Hopefully, by then the flies will have flown.

Love,
Mairi

~

19 May

Dear Gran,

Today is even sunnier, like summer. I watch the turquoise sea glint like sequinned satin, and listen to the waves whisper against the pebble shore. The air smells of sun, seaweed and coconut sunscreen. Children giggle, seagulls chatter overhead.

Women wear mini dresses so short they air the cellulite on their buttocks, and shirtless men show still-white beer bellies.

I'm drinking cloudy lemonade, great stuff which tastes of real lemons. I'm on my third big glass already. The sun makes the ice cubes in the glass sparkle like jewels.

Although I have a beach towel and bikini in my bag, I postpone the sunbathing, because those insects seem to like bare, salt-sticky skin. Today, it's not just black flies, but longish insects with curling, twitching tails. They actually bite. Not that it hurts, it's just a tiny stab, but there are so many.

I think I'll put on my cardigan, although that's crazy in the heat. I guess there's no such thing as a perfect day. There's always a fly in the ointment, or a bug in the cream. I couldn't have cream with tea today; those crawlies would land on the scones and that would ruin my appetite. They're absolutely everywhere.

Considering the weird weather in recent months, it's normal. Winter wasn't cold enough to kill off insect larvae, and the chilly spring delayed their hatching. Now they've all hatched at once.

Tomorrow, I'll wear a loose-fitting cotton blouse with long sleeves, more comfortable in this heat than a cardigan. And I think I'll wear trainers, with socks, so the bugs will stop creeping between my toes.

Those crawlies come from everywhere, as if attracted to my wrists and face and I can scarcely brush them off. They're all over this letter, too, like splashes of black ink. They cling, so I can't blow them away, and when I brush them off, they leave dark smears. I started this letter several times on fresh paper, but I'm giving up. You'll forgive a few stains, won't you?

Love,
Mairi

~

20 May
Dear Gran,

According to YahooUK, yesterday was the hottest ever day in Britain in May for over three hundred years!

Today is even hotter. The heat has boiled all the colour

out of the sea and sky, so they're a featureless pale blue. The asphalt turns liquid, the metal tables glare. Insects are everywhere.

Most people have fled indoors. I wouldn't mind the heat – you know me, I'm a sun worshipper – but those insects are annoying. I thought they'd be gone by now, but no, they're still here, fat and black and creepy.

It's icky to have them crawl on the table and drop into my drink, so I gave up and came in. Actually, I like it inside. The place has an olde-worlde feel, with framed samplers on the walls and embroidered tablecloths, and it's pleasant to sit beside the ventilator blowing a cool breeze. I ordered that delicious cloudy lemonade, but they've sold out. The waitress says they've sold out of ginger beer too, and of ginger ale and diet coke and everything cold. So I'm having Earl Grey tea, and I feel like a Victorian spinster sipping from my flowery porcelain cup.

I was about to write about the relief of sitting in a bug-free zone, but there's a fat one crawling along the edge of the saucer right now. I'll ask the waitress to take the saucer away, with the bug on it, and bring me a fresh one.

It's shaped like a miniature scorpion with wings. It seems to make a sound, like a faint *cleck-cleck-cleck*, but it's hard to hear with the clattering crockery and the humming coffee maker.

I've never seen this type of insect before. Or maybe I have seen it, but never noticed. I don't usually watch bugs. It's just the sheer mass of them that draws my attention.

Maybe it's a species that hatches not every year, only if it's unusually hot in May. From this description, do you recall this type from your childhood?

Love,
Mairi

~

21 May

Dear Gran,

Yesterday was the hottest recorded temperature in British weather history, ever! Everyone's moaning and complaining. You know the English, they're never content with the weather, and close to panic whenever the weather is in the least out of the ordinary. Other countries have hotter weather all year round, but the BBC advises people in the southeast to drink plenty of liquids, stay indoors and avoid exertion.

Me, I'd happily stay on the beach soaking up the heat. It's only those insects that make me stay home today. I even keep the windows shut, which is a nuisance in this heat. I wish I could let air breeze through my flat, but I don't want those black bugs to creep in.

My theory is that they came in tourist luggage from Brazil or Bahrain or Bangladesh, then hibernated for years, until the extremely warm weather cued them to hatch.

Their bites don't swell, but they leave red wounds, as if they had taken flesh. Have you ever heard of insects doing that?

YahooUK News says the heat wave in the southeast has stimulated 'unusual insect activity', and shows a video about beetles caught outside London – allegedly a species believed extinct since the Middle Ages. One entomologist declares insect larvae can lie dormant for centuries until conditions are right, another disputes this. Most commenters say it's a hoax, but most of the comments are from Americans, and they would say that.

That was the explanation, I thought – but it isn't. The London bug is round and brown; not like the one we have here. Of course, London is seventy miles away, so different things may happen there. Wouldn't it be crazy if the heat had revived two separate extinct species?

More likely, this is just the normal kind of insect we

always have in May, and just never really noticed it because they don't usually appear en masse. Maybe the heat has made them grow bigger than usual?

I found a twitch-tail crawling on the kitchen floor. I didn't see it at first. There was just this weird *cleck-cleck-cleck* noise coming from somewhere, and when I followed it to its source, there was this fat black thing crawling out from under the fridge. It was the biggest one I'd seen, two inches at least, the tail curled and twitched, the wings flapped, and all the while it made *cleck-cleck-cleck-cleck*, quite loud.

How it got in with all the windows closed, I have no idea, but I squashed it.

I hope you're well in Scotland, and don't get any funny bugs there.

Love,
Mairi

~

22 May.
Dear Gran,
You're lucky the heat is only in the southeast, and you're cool in Scotland. Yes, the heat is getting too intense even for me.

Strangely, apart from a brief mention of the London bug, none of the news channels mention insects, so maybe this outbreak is just in our town.

When I walked to the letterbox, I wore a balaclava and gloves - you'd have laughed to see me in this heat - and still bugs crawled into my clothes and bit. Anyway, I kept my promise to write every day.

Black creatures cover the windows, some as long as my thumb. The sun comes through only in small patches, when their tails twitch. And they make this clacking noise which is really creepy coming from so many of them. The windows are double glazed, and I can hear it through both panes.

I wish the greedy local seagulls would hunt these bugs. They normally gobble up everything, but they seem uninterested. Let's hope these bugs mature soon and fly to wherever they belong.

I watched the biggest devour a ladybird, one of the pretty red ones with seven black dots. It was ghastly to watch, but I couldn't look away. Such big teeth. I didn't realise that bugs had teeth. Is bugs the correct word? Are they insects at all?

If this gets worse, I may not be able to go to the postbox tomorrow. Of course I'll try, but if I have to miss a day, I hope you'll forgive me.

I'm googling as I write this. 'Insect, black, long tail' brings thousands of images, but nothing remotely like these crawlies.

The nearest in shape is a fossilised creature from prehistory, a sharp-toothed predator with wings and elongated, curving tail. But this can't be it - it's four feet long. Anyway, it's prehistoric. Although that entomologist said insects can hatch after eight hundred years, surely they couldn't after eighty million … Could they?

Love,
Mairi

FURZBY HOLT

Jonathan Broughton

"**P**ick up, Sandra!" Kevin flung the mobile onto the passenger seat. "See if I care!" But he did care and he ground his teeth. *And* he'd forgotten to bring his hands-free kit. At least out here no CCTV recorded his crime.

Where was Furzby Holt? The satnav hadn't spoken for miles. The orange arrow rested on the green line which stretched to infinity against a grey background.

Queen's 'Bohemian Rhapsody' trilled from his mobile. Sandra! At last and he pressed the first button that made contact with his thumb. "Look – it's ok, no need to say sorry, but …"

"I should hope not," replied a male voice. "Where the hell are you?"

Oh God! Mr Richards, his boss. "On my way, Mr Richards."

"You mean you haven't even got there yet?"

The bare horizon stretched before him. "It's further than I thought."

"That's because you started late," barked Mr Richards. "What's the excuse this time? No, let me guess, your watch stopped."

"I'm going as fast as I can." Lame but true.

"I want those census forms at my front door by ten tonight. Or do I have to come out there and collect them myself?"

Kevin flicked the satnav. The picture didn't change and the voice stayed silent. "I'll do my best."

"You'll do better than that."

"I'll get them to you ..." The line went dead. "Mr Richards?"

He brought the car to a shuddering halt and the satnav's orange arrow melted into the green line and disappeared.

He unclipped his belt and pushed himself out of the car. Why didn't people post their census forms back like they were told? He rummaged through the junk in his boot and hooked out his road atlas. Why did he have to go traipsing round the country like a nanny?

The sharp retort as he slammed the boot lid alerted him to the silence. He noticed his surroundings for the first time since he had stepped out of the car. Beds of reed marsh stretched away on either side for as far as the eye could see. The breeze ruffled their feathery tops and whistled a low note through their stalks. The western horizon blazed orange from the setting sun and the eastern sky darkened with the approach of night.

Kreeeee! A small bird rose vertically from the reeds.

No traffic on the road. Road? Big word for the narrow strip of asphalt that was barely wide enough to let two cars pass. He squinted. What was that? Like a smudge against the sky, far ahead on the horizon. Were they trees, or houses? Could it be Furzby Holt?

He flicked the pages of his atlas. East Sussex, between Hastings and Winchelsea, the B - the B what? A thin beige line edged with dashes stretched towards the coast. It wasn't even listed as a B road, it was a track. It stopped millimetres from the English Channel and there in brackets was the name, Furzby Holt.

That smudge must be it. He flung the atlas onto the passenger seat and put his foot down.

Why didn't Sandra return his calls? Twenty minutes ago he had asked her why she was cooling off. All right, he blurted it out, it wasn't tactful, frustration made his tongue flap. She accused *him* for her behaviour. He only wanted her for one thing, she shouted, and he wasn't very good at that.

The insults flew like fists. It was a spat, all couples had them. He loved her, he told her that. Right now they should be making up.

The smudge ahead defined itself into trees of different heights. No sign of any houses or a flicker of light amongst the shadows. Please ... let this be the right place. He needed to get back to Sandra, time spent on explaining who said what and why was such a waste.

He flicked on his headlights. The white beam hit the road and a mass of black night that came hurtling straight towards him.

The rolling dark hit the car with a loud thud and a piercing screech tore the air.

The blackness rolled across the bonnet and cannoned into the windscreen. In the confusion of images, an open blood-red mouth with yellow teeth pierced his mind and lingered.

"No!" He squealed to a halt. The car slewed sideways and the creature rolled off.

His breath came in shaking gasps as he clenched and unclenched the wheel.

No screams of pain, but his heart thudded in his ears so loud that it drowned out any other noise. A glance in the mirror revealed a red glow on the road from his rear lights, but no sign of anyone or anything lying there injured. He

wound down the driver's window and the cool air fanned
his burning cheeks. The car engine idly ticking over was the
only sound.

Whatever it was lay further back on the road, or in the
ditch, and needed help. That red mouth, those yellow teeth.
His chest pricked with sweat. Just the dusk and his
headlights, that explained its strangeness, but he didn't want
to look at it again.

He slammed his foot down and forced the back wheels
into a spin. Thank goodness there were no witnesses.

He flicked the beam to full and drove at a steady thirty
miles per hour. His thumping heart subsided to a dull thud
and his breathing deepened. The dashboard clock flicked to
eight p.m. He thought about the job, not the accident.

The computer printout listed just thirteen houses in
Furzby Holt. He reckoned on an hours' work to collect the
forms, taking into consideration reluctant homeowners
telling him why they hadn't filled it in, people who had lost
them and empty homes because the occupants were out for
the evening. Barring any major delays, he should be back in
Hastings and at Mr Richard's front door well before ten.

The car bumped and lurched and he slowed to fifteen
miles per hour. Smooth asphalt had deteriorated to dry pot-
holed earth.

The trees towered above him. Beyond, the sea
reflected the clear sky with the lightest shade of turquoise.
Furzby Holt benefited from being in a cool setting, in nice
weather. In winter the storms must be hell, all the trees
leant at various angles towards the east.

The car rolled and he eased down to five miles an
hour. The last thing he wanted was a puncture or broken
suspension.

Then he spotted the wooden huts under the trees. This
place didn't even have houses! His heart sank, for the huts

stood in random disorder. How could he keep track of the numbers in the dark? Did he have the torch?

He slowed to a halt and extracted the computer printout from his case. What was the sequence of house numbers? He scowled, for dashes occupied the spaces where there should be numbers. All he had to go on were people's names.

He didn't take this into consideration in his carefully planned timing scheme. Any residence without a number required detailed criteria before agency standards confirmed the occupants authentic. Why didn't he see this earlier? If he had, that row with Sandra would never have happened. He thumped his fist on the wheel, switched off the engine and climbed out of the car.

The leaves rustled in the breeze and a branch creaked. Long grass grew in clumps and trembled in the keen air. No obvious paths linked the huts, and the ground was more sand than earth. No one was about.

A tattered red curtain hung at the window of the nearest hut. No flick or twitch to indicate that he was being watched. Had he been spotted approaching through the reed beds? Had someone witnessed his collision? Wondering wasted time, if anyone asked he'd say he'd hit a rabbit.

He opened the boot and rooted round for the torch. He found it, shook it and heard the batteries rattle, but when he switched it on nothing happened. He flung it back and slammed the lid.

The shadows deepened as he approached the nearest door. Dark green paint, faded and flaked, exposed grey planks that had dried and cracked. He took a deep breath.

Then, that terrible shriek rose again across the reeds and he cowered from shock. It was still alive, the 'thing' had followed him.

"No need to be frightened."

He spun round and rammed his back against the door.
A woman, bent double, her face hidden by a hooded cloak,
stood just feet away. She held an old fashioned lantern
which shone with a soft yellow glow. He hadn't heard her,
hadn't even sensed that she was behind him.

"He is hunting. He will not trouble you while I am
here." Her voice quivered as if the breeze blew out of her
mouth. Shapeless garments covered her thin frame and her
feet, which were bare, exposed more bone than flesh. "Why
have you come?"

"I've … I've come to collect the census forms." He
reached into his jacket pocket and extracted his plastic ID
card. "What do you mean … hunting? What is it?"

"Census forms?" She spoke the words slowly as if they
were foreign.

He waved them at her. "It's to keep a record of how
many people live in the UK, where they live, what their
work is. Haven't you seen it on television? A Snapshot of
Britain …" He faltered, not a single hut had a satellite dish.
Did mains electricity even run to Furzby Holt?

She shuffled closer and a thin hand emerged from
under the tattered edges of her shawl and took the papers.

"They were posted to you a month ago." He peered at
the track behind him, shadows criss-crossed its pale
surface. There was no obvious movement, but it was hard
to see.

The old lady held the forms close to her hooded face
and lifted the lantern to see by its light. "Posted? No post
comes to Furzby Holt," she whispered. "Nothing ever
comes here." The forms trembled in her shaking fingers.
"No one ever comes here. And those that do, never leave."

His stomach tightened. "What … what do you mean?"
He glanced at the reeds.

She turned the first page of the top form. "There are
names." She ran her finger down the agency list slotted

behind the cover. Beside each name was a box to tick for absent householders. Kevin considered ticking every single one and getting out of there as fast as possible.

"Henry Gavell." She peered closer. "Morweena Atkins, Sybil Pettigrew ... I did not know that these names were remembered."

He frowned. "Well ... yes. Names are only removed from the registry when the person dies."

She nodded and the movement was like the slow rise and fall of a heavy weight. "This *census* believes they are alive?"

"Of course." The hairs stood up on the back of his neck. "Aren't they?"

She pulled the hood away from her face with slow care. The thin material dropped in folds across her shoulders. She was almost bald, the long wisps of hair that remained gleamed snow white. Wrinkles, many and deep, lined a face that looked dry as paper. Her thin nose, hooked like an old fashioned witch's he remembered from story books, sprouted tufts of nasal hair and black eyes glimmered from under heavy lids.

"Yes," she answered slowly. "They live." Then her tone hardened. "And these papers prove it." She reached under her shawl and pulled out a wooden whistle that dangled at the end of a leather cord.

She put it to her mouth, pursed her lips and blew. The note was not shrill, as Kevin expected, but soft with a dull and hollow sound. She blew it three times and then let it drop.

He attempted to take the papers off her. "I don't need to trouble you any longer."

She flicked them out of his reach. "Wait. They come."

The peeling door beside him shuddered and opened. Rusted hinges grated and the doors in the other huts opened too, as if joining in some jarring chorus.

Sweat prickled Kevin's back. He tensed, ready to run, but the old lady gripped his arm. Her hold was tight and her sharp fingers dug into his skin. "Do not fear, you will come to no harm. Not while I am here."

He did fear, very much, but her grip squeezed tighter at each attempt to pull away.

Beyond the door, something shuffled, accompanied by a gurgling, wheezing rasp and a figure lurched into view.

Brown skin hung in clumps and shreds from a skeletal frame. Yellow eyes stared, mad-seeming and unfocused. Strands of long hair hung in greasy coils across its face and the stink that clouded around it was of dead things left for too long in the air.

Kevin covered his nose as his stomach heaved.

The thing opened its mouth. Two green teeth dangled from fibrous strands of puss-white skin. "Nnng arng nng arung gunng."

"Good evening, Captain Loftus." The old lady raised her lantern in greeting. "We have a visitor."

Captain Loftus twisted and gazed at Kevin.

"He's come for the *census*." She still said the word as if it were new-made.

"Oh, God …" Kevin gasped.

"I'm afraid he won't be able to help you here." She gave a chuckle. "Many have called on his name before, to no effect."

"Let me go!" He wrenched and jerked with all the strength in his trembling arms as he tried to break free.

"Please calm down." A stone deep-set in hard earth could not have held him so fast. "I don't expect you've seen his like before, have you?" Her wrinkled face cracked into a wide grin. "Not many people are granted that pleasure. You're one of the lucky ones."

"Oh *please*, I can't stand it. Let me go." Tears wet his face and his body jolted as if hit by electric shocks. His knees shook. If he fell … he thought of Sandra and not the waiting darkness.

"I don't know why you're making such a fuss," the old lady scolded. "We want to help."

The horror raised and lowered its arms. "Nunnng gung hnng nunngn."

"Are you going to shake his hand?" the old lady asked. "He's welcoming you to our little village."

The stench of sewers hit the back of Kevin's throat. The old lady let go of his arm and he crumpled onto all fours. He could no more run than fly.

She squatted beside him, placed the lantern on the ground and sifted through the census forms. "There are questions and empty squares beside them. Is that for writing? My writing is bad. I learnt my letters when I was a girl, but I cannot remember the order they go in to write words." She thrust the papers under his nose. "You will read and we will answer. Do you have ink and nib?"

Through Kevin's tears, the papers blurred and yet the census forms offered some hope of sanity. He could ask the questions that he knew so well. He could write the answers that required brief explanations. He could do all that, that was normal, and this familiarity reached out to him like a lifeline. His tears lessened and he pushed himself up into a sitting position. Cross-legged, head bowed, he pulled a biro from his pocket and took the papers. He imagined Mr Richard's reaction, but his boss's anger was nothing compared to this nightmare.

"Who's first?" demanded the old lady. She slid the lamp closer.

Kevin wiped his eyes and squinted at the topmost name. "Henry Gavell."

"Henry?" the old lady called. "Come here."

In a semi-circle, shuffling from foot to foot as if uncertain of their balance, stood many figures half-seen in the dim light. All of them as wasted and rotten as the captain. The stink of foetid decay swept across the clearing in waves. One figure limped forward, its mouth hung slack and an eye rolled on its cheek as it dangled from a sliver of membrane.

"This is Henry," said the old lady. "You'll have to speak up because he's lost his ears."

Kevin gazed at the form, the words swirled as if floating in water. He shut his eyes, squeezed hard, and opened them again. His hand shook as he wrote. 'Henry Gavell.'

He read out the first question. "How many people live in your house?" His voice swooped between high and low registers.

"Ahrngng."

Kevin held the pen poised over the box. What?

"One," replied the old lady. "His wife died in eighteen eighty-three, before I arrived."

Eighteen eighty-three? Kevin wrote 'one' in the box. He breathed through his mouth to lessen the pungent earth-smell pulsing off Henry Gavell. "What type of accommodation does your household occupy?" He read the list. "Detached, semi-detached, linked by a garage ..." This was crazy and he skipped the rest until he reached the bottom: "A caravan or other temporary mobile structure?"

"Caravan?" questioned the old lady. Kevin didn't have the strength to explain, but he didn't have to as she announced, "Call it a cabin. That's right isn't it, Henry?"

"Mnnng."

How long was this going to take? No way would he finish before ten. The missed deadline meant a financial penalty deducted from his wages. That presumed that when he had finished they let him go. The old lady sat alert and attentive as if she enjoyed this unlooked for distraction. He had no choice but to continue.

"Do ... you have ... any of the long standing conditions ..." he stuttered. "Deafness or severe hearing impediment?"

"Deaf as a post aren't you, Henry?" chortled the old lady.

"Blindness or severe visual impairment?"

She nudged his arm. "Look at him." But he didn't look, he just ticked the box.

"A condition that limits walking, climbing stairs, lifting or carrying?"

"Well," the old crone pondered, "all of those."

Kevin ticked the box and the next two for 'Learning Difficulty,' and 'A Long-standing Psychological or Emotional Condition.' He smoothed the paper. "What do you consider your national identity to be?"

The old lady frowned.

Kevin read the list. "Welsh, Scottish, Northern Irish, Irish ..."

"We are all the same here," and she waved her arm in a languid sweep towards the shuffling figures.

"British?" suggested Kevin.

"English," she replied.

He wiped the cooling sweat from his brow. "Income." The list in these circumstances was mad. "Perhaps I don't need to read these."

"Money?" queried the old lady. Kevin nodded.

"Read it," she insisted. "We liked money once, didn't we?"

A chorus of "Mngannmgana" rumbled round the clearing.

"State Benefits," he began.

The old lady stopped him. "What is that?"

"You know: income support, housing benefits, jobseekers allowance."

She glanced from him to the forms and back again, puzzled.

"If you can't find a job," his voice wavered. "Then the state hands out payments to help you through."

"If you can't find a job," she repeated, "then this *state* gives you money?" Her childish surprise made it sound ridiculous.

"That's right," he replied.

"You mean ..." Her eyes narrowed. "We can get *paid* for being like this?"

An image of Henry Gavell shambling into the local Jobcentre almost made him laugh. But it was the laughter of hysteria which, once released, threatened insanity. "Well ... yes, I suppose so ... if you can't work."

A high-pitched shriek tore across the reed beds and Kevin burst into a drenching sweat. Whatever it was sounded close and angry.

The mob gurgled and moaned. Those with eyes stared into the dark and a few shuffled towards the dirt track. The old lady reached for her whistle and blew a single long note.

"Nngmnngnng." The shambling few halted.

"The time to feed is close," she called. "But not yet, not quite yet."

Kevin trembled and yet a glance at the old lady revealed no malice directed towards him. The tension in his shoulders made his neck ache.

"Mad Jack." She pointed to a name on the list, but Kevin's eyes refused to focus. "Mad and bad in life," she muttered. "And mad and bad in ... well, he's still mad and bad." Her eyes dimmed as if lost in thought.

Kevin's tongue rolled like some alien implant in his mouth. What did these *things* feast on? Why did they have to wait? Why did Mad Jack keep screaming and how had he survived the impact with the car?

"Continue." The old lady's abrupt command forced his concentration back onto the census form.

He swallowed hard and his tongue moistened. "That's … that's the last question," he lied. "It just has to be signed." He held the form up, but looked at the sandy ground.

"Mnnngmng."

The old lady snatched it from his hand. "Give it here. Henry lost his fingers when he jammed them in the door." She stared at the form. "Where do I write?"

Kevin pointed to the box on the first page. She took his pen and scrawled a big 'X.'

"That's you done, Henry." She thrust the form and the pen back at Kevin. "You can fill in the others, young man. They are all exactly the same as Henry's. Only …" She squinted at the figures at the edge of the lantern's light. "Ruby Monks. She has a baby. Called it Matthew. Ruby love, where are you?"

Kevin peered sideways, afraid to look, but curiosity overcame his fear. A figure approached and clasped against its chest was a bundle of bones held together by thin strips of yellow tendon. No skin or hair covered the skull and its tiny jaw hung slack. Out of its mouth dribbled brown sand.

Kevin spun away and retched. The old lady's voice topped his heaving gasps. "Don't leave out Matthew. He's the only baby we have."

These – creatures – had kids? Madness jabbered at the fringes of his mind and he clutched his head as if that might keep the insanity out. When he looked up, a smile creased the old lady's thin lips as she gazed back with a rueful glance. A wistful note tinged her voice.

"There is one name missing. Mine: Tabitha Critchell."

He didn't know what to say and his ragged breath wheezed.

"I lived in Rye, perhaps my name is there." She shuffled onto her knees, placed a hand on Kevin's shoulder and stood. "They cast me out. Accused me of ... bad habits." She chuckled. "Blinkered they were, scared of what I had to offer." She covered her head with her shawl. "I found my way here. I was taken in, made welcome." She stooped and picked up the lantern. "These are my friends. I've kept them - alive - all these years, my gift to them in thanks." She waved the lantern and the light flickered around the clearing and the shadows leapt and darted through the trees. "I am old. There is no one to save me. When I die, what will happen? Who will look after them?" Kevin didn't meet her gaze, and she bent closer. "Happiness together like this is precious."

Her hand rested on his head and she stroked his hair. "Tonight has been a surprise for both of us." Her touch scared him, though each stroke was gentle. "For you have the proof that we are not forgotten. Perhaps, after all these years there might also be forgiveness?"

She hooked her hand under his arm and pulled. He scrabbled in the dirt until he stood on shaking legs.

She held the lantern close to his face. "Return to this *state* and tell them. Let them come and see. How can they know that we mean no harm if they daren't look?"

A distant scream echoed into the night sky and Tabitha's grip tightened. "My strength is failing. Mad Jack will break free. He senses my ailing powers. He has no love, even though I saved him from death. He will be the first to feed on my corpse and then the others will follow."

Kevin, aware of being pushed, but not sensing any movement in his legs, stumbled against the car. His surprise at touching cold metal cleared his mind and relief flooded his chest. He scrabbled with the handle and wrenched the door open.

Tabitha released his arm. "Furzby Holt, remember that name."

He slammed the door. The keys jangled in the ignition as he forced his shaking fingers to grip. The engine roared into life. He flicked the lights to full beam and the clearing lit up.

The creatures lifted their arms. Tattered skin trembled, empty eye sockets gazed blank and black and rotten teeth gleamed green.

Kevin locked the wheel hard right and put his foot down. Fear ignored common sense as he rattled and bounced along the dirt track. Shadows sprang through the reed beds as he sped past and pebbles pinged off the car's metal.

A figure leapt out of the ditch in front of him, arms raised, legs splayed, wide eyes red and staring as it pounced. Its open mouth peeled back as vicious as a hunting carnivore.

The instinct to avoid a collision snagged Kevin's fear and he braked. Too late, he realised his mistake as the figure leapt onto the bonnet and smashed its face against the windscreen. Split and jagged teeth snapped, hands like claws, their twisted nails sharp as talons, tore away the wipers. Then, bunched into fists, they hammered on the glass. With a crack, it splintered and a probing finger forced a hole and twisted towards Kevin's face.

"No!" He wrenched the wheel left, hit the accelerator and, bent double to see through the unbroken bottom of the windscreen, sped forwards in a series of jerks. The figure rolled and bucked on the bonnet. It banged its head against the windscreen again and again, showering Kevin with broken glass.

He thrust his foot down, the car leapt forward and the figure lost its grip and dropped off the bonnet.

The windscreen caved in and the night air blew into Kevin's face like a gale. The track levelled to a smoother surface and he went faster. A cry of impotent rage, louder than the rush of wind and the engine's roar, followed him as he sped away.

He didn't slow down until he approached the main road, where he took the census forms, held them above the empty window frame, and let go. He watched them in his mirror as they fluttered like broken birds and vanished into the dark.

He indicated left as he turned off the track and headed for Hastings. The streaming wind hurt his eyes.

A car coming towards him dipped its headlights and the right indicator flashed. As he passed he glanced sideways and saw a man with both hands gripped high on the wheel and his head bent forward as he peered through thick-lensed glasses. Mr Richards!

Kevin snapped his foot onto the brake, but he winced, his eyes dazzled by a lorry's high lights reflecting off his mirror as it bore down on him from behind. He accelerated, no layby existed on this stretch of road for him to pull over. He patted the passenger seat, feeling for his mobile, but broken glass scratched his palm. The next roundabout was on the outskirts of Hastings, still ten minutes away. Where was his phone? Then it rang and his heart jumped. It wasn't on the seat, but in his jacket pocket and he fumbled one-handed past the jacket flap to reach it. He jabbed a button with his thumb and pressed the phone hard against his ear.

"Mr Richards?" The wind howled. "Where are you?"

"Hi babe, it's me. Look, I'm really, really sorry."

"Sandra … Sandra …" And as she spoke, tears of relief streamed down Kevin's face. He put his foot down and raced away from Furzby Holt.

Out here, thank goodness, there were no witnesses.

SCRUPLES

Rayne Hall

"A chance like this won't come again, Alditha," I urge. "We will be rich."

Wind whines against the walls and rattles the shutters. This year of Our Lord 1287 has brought more storms than I have seen I have seen in my life.

Alditha fingers the barbette under her chin. "Yes, but John ... isn't stealing a sin?"

"This isn't a time for scruples. Do you want to gut fish for the rest of your life?"

I place a slice of cold venison on her trencher and watch her eyes widen. As a harbour fishmonger, she has never tasted meat. What I have shown her tonight has whet her desire for a finer life: the fresh rushes on the floor, the tapestries keeping out the winter chill, the dried flowers hanging from the rafters, the wax candles fragrant with the scent of honey. When she raises the wine goblet to her lips, her face glazes as if she is tasting paradise.

The house jolts as another rock breaks from the cliff and crashes into the sea. Alditha snaps out of her bliss and crosses herself. "John, this isn't right. I shouldn't be here. We shouldn't be doing this."

I've waited for years for this chance, and I will not let Alditha spoil it.

Master De Coucy and the family have gone away

visiting, and taken the maids with them, leaving me – their trusted steward – in charge. Their wealth is waiting to be carried off, and Alditha is the perfect helpmeet, or so it seemed when I first told her of my plan. Then, she was as keen as I, but tonight, her fear-pale face is flushing with guilt. I thought she possessed a ruthless streak. Was I mistaken? I must find a way to bring her ruthlessness to life.

This is the first time she sits in a chair, since the common folk in their harbour huts own no furniture, and from the way she strokes the carved armrests, I can tell she likes the comfort.

I stoke this glimmer of greed into bright flames. "One day you will own a chair, and candles like these, real wax. You'll eat meat every feast day, at least four times every year. You'll wear the finest wool, and your surcoat will be of embroidered velvet."

"Oh, John, this will be so good." Her eyes light with dreamy desire, then darken with concern. "When they come home and see their things are gone, won't they be hurt?"

"Don't worry about it. They are so rich, they can buy new things and will barely feel the loss." When she frowns in disbelief, I give her a reassuring smile. "Trust your future husband."

I gather the selected items, pieces of modest weight and great value, easily sold – the gilded candlesticks, the finest tapestries, the casket of spices – and stuff them into the sack for Alditha to carry away. When Master De Coucy returns, he will find his home robbed, and his trusted steward gagged, bound and beaten.

The wind picks up, slaps against the walls like wet sheets. Another jolt shudders through the cliff, followed by a crash. Alditha pales, crosses herself again. "John, what if this is a sign from heaven that what we're doing is wrong?"

Will those scruples never cease? "Rockfalls happen all the time," I assure her. "If you lived on the cliff, you'd be used to them."

She frowns, probably thinking of the storm in February, when the sea hollowed the sandstone cliff so much that a whole section of it collapsed. But we're safe here, so close to the castle.

Pressing ahead with my plan, I kneel on the wooden floor and hold my hands together behind me. "Tie me up. Tighter. Real robbers wouldn't be kind. I must be uncomfortable for the night." The chafing rope bites into my wrists, then my ankles, and the short rope between hands and feet pulls my back into a painful arch. When de Coucy finds me, he'll see real suffering in my face. But it needs more. "Beat me. I need bruises."

"I don't want to hurt you, John." She gives me a few feeble slaps with her slipper.

"Harder, harder!" I urge, spurring the ruthlessness I know she has in her. "Think of the life you will lead! The candles, the dresses, the meat, the chair! Now put the gag into my mouth."

My link with Alditha is unknown. No one will suspect a fishmonger in cahoots with the steward of a fine house, or search her harbour hut for silver. On a stormy night like this, nobody is out in the street, especially not on the clifftop at Hastings. Huddled in their houses, the neighbours won't see Alditha lug away a big sack of loot.

As I lie curled on the rushes, Alditha hoists the sack, but hesitates once more.

Another jolt cracks like the lash of a gigantic whip. The whole house judders, shakes, roars. The last jolt uproots us, breaks the house into two. The candles go out. Icy wind slams into my back, but the gag swallows my scream.

More than half the house has crashed into the sea, and

I lie on the edge of the abyss.

The floor rushes hit me, then get sucked into the void. I must get away from the edge or I will fall hundreds of feet into the howling darkness. I try to crawl to safety, but can scarcely wiggle with my hands and feet bound behind my back.

Alditha clings to a tapestry on the landward wall, staring in open-mouthed horror through the near darkness. I want to yell at her to untie me, to pull me to safety, but the gag permits a mere gargle. The storm roars like trumpets and cymbals on Judgement Day.

As I roll my eyes to convey my despair, she stays by the wall, as if fear has nailed her to the spot.

Then the wind drops. Into the sudden silence, a seagull screeches. Waves crash below, timber creaks around me, and my heart thuds. A stone breaks under my arm. I hear its scraping crumble, the clattering and finally the splash.

At last, she comes. Good girl, I knew she would not leave me lying on the edge. Her steps are cautious, testing the ground, as she overcomes her fears.

With my eyes, I try to reassure her, to tell her that fate is on our side. De Coucy will assume the treasures have fallen with the house, and I with it, never suspecting the truth. Alditha and I will leave tonight, make our way to London, sell our treasures, begin a comfortable life.

The corners of her mouth turn up. Her eyes narrow and gleam. Her streak of ruthlessness is asserting itself. I wait for her to bend to undo the knots. Instead, she smiles coldly.

"This is no time for scruples." Her slippered foot pushes against my chest. "I will be rich."

DEMON ALCOHOL

Mark Cassell

Tammy clutched the banister and lowered herself to the first stair. Each step sent thunder to her head. The further she descended, the louder the sound of tinkling cutlery … which also threatened to split her skull. Voices drifted up towards her, arguing perhaps. And that smell of an English breakfast tugged her stomach.

As she reached the bottom, she considered the front door, fresh air, a walk along the beach.

After last night's heavy drinking session, she wondered if she honestly could handle any food. This being their first morning on a well-deserved coastal break, they had not had a chance to sample the Bed and Breakfast's food. Greg was still snug in bed with a burning sunrise pushing against the drawn curtains.

He'd only grunted at her when she'd told him she needed food.

She loved him to bits but often his only response would be that grunt, whether he was sleepy or not. It bugged the hell out of her. That said, she recognised she was the talker in the relationship and she guessed that was why they worked well together. Wasn't that the way with most couples?

Last night however, overlooking a tranquil sea from the quaint pub where they'd necked all that gin – and rum – they'd talked each other's ears off, covering everything from God and politics to fuel prices and whether he should get that cut on his hand actually seen to.

It was nasty. He'd done it when they'd first arrived.

Men. Macho twats. All of them.

Greg was no different.

Emerging from the bathroom with a towel wrapped around his mid-section, he'd ducked beneath a wooden rafter that divided the ceiling. The smell of shower gel and deodorant wafted in with him.

She sat on the end of the four-poster bed, pulling on her tights and watched him reach up and grip the top of the beam. Muscles flexing he pulled his legs back so his shins were parallel with the carpet, and began a set of pull-ups. One … two … three. He was a show-off without doubt, but she didn't mind; he put a lot of hard work in the gym.

Four … five …

After several more, he levelled his feet and let go. Both heels thumped the floor. He sucked air between clenched teeth and grabbed his wrist, glaring at it.

"What?" she asked.

The muscles along his jaw wriggled. His eyes were tiny.

She stood and approached him. "What is it?"

He ducked beneath another beam to meet her in the centre of the room.

"What did you do?" she demanded.

"Fucking nail," he said and actually smiled.

Blood trickled between his fingers.

"Let me see." She gently moved his hand away.

Running with the veins along his wrist a ragged hole gaped, oozing blood. A graze zigzagged up his forearm like a lightning strike.

"Deep." She knew she didn't need to tell him that.

She'd then spent the next five minutes nursing the dopey bastard.

Now, Tammy headed towards an oak door where she assumed breakfast was being served. Given the layout of the place, it had to lead to the dining room – she couldn't remember their brief tour given by the owner, a grey-haired lady with a wrinkled face and bright eyes.

Tammy's shoes clipped the tiles, bouncing echoes off the wood-panels either side of her. She failed to make out what the voices were saying. The dining room sounded packed; she certainly hadn't realised there were so many guests. The clanking of glassware and cutlery intensified. She wrapped her cardigan tighter and hugged herself, convinced she saw her breath plume. Still the sounds of breakfast got louder, and—

The noises, and those voices, ceased. Snapped off as though by a switch. Silence pulled her to a stop where a wall-mounted lamp flickered. The wooden panels, aged and gouged in places, seemed to close in, to squeeze as that sudden hush lengthened. She pressed a hand against a panel, if only to steady herself. Its rough surface chilled her clammy palm.

Again, the sound of chinking cutlery continued.

She breathed out, long and loud.

Silence once more.

Her heartbeat throbbed between her ears, renewing the fuzz and thump of the hangover. She dared her feet to move. Her toes twitched. That was all. Silently she screamed at them. Two more steps to the door, come on…

Eventually her feet, her legs, obeyed.

Deep gouges surrounded the iron knob, but the door was ajar. The hinges squealed as she pushed it inward.

Darkness.

No one.

Her head pounded.

Silence and shadows hugged all corners of the room, the dining table empty, neither plate nor cutlery laid out. This made no sense. Beyond the table was the kitchen which remained in an even deeper gloom. The smell of bacon and eggs became something sweeter, putrid. Like sewage.

She winced and stepped back.

The beach seemed a better place to be right then. Her mind was playing tricks for sure. She turned.

Sounds.

Again.

A cold sweat prickled her spine.

From the dining room, now behind her, cutlery clattered on a plate as though someone threw a fork or knife. A glass tinkled, perhaps even cracked. Someone laughed: a man or a woman, Tammy had no idea.

She spun round.

Again, no one.

Only … had the room darkened further? She couldn't even make out where the dining table was, let alone the kitchen beyond.

A floorboard creaked. A sharp, echoing crack on that black silence.

She lurched sideways and her arm smacked the door frame.

She was alone, dammit. No one there.

Her heart punched her ribcage, repeatedly urging her to get out, leave this place. But she darted for the staircase instead. Was Greg up yet? If he wasn't, she'd wake him. They'd grab their stuff and leave. They didn't have to stay here, they *mustn't* stay here. They had to get far away from this place. It was haunted. Or something.

Not her imagination.

Bounding up the stairs two at a time, every footfall slamming agony into her brain, she reached the top step. Heading along the landing, she passed the other rooms.

So quiet.

Above and behind her, the lights buzzed and winked out. One by one along the hallway. *Clink*. Buzz and then *clink*. Another. Then another.

A twilight blue swamped the hallway like it was 4 a.m. *Clink*.

Outside their room, the key caught in her pocket. She yanked it free and it fell from jelly fingers. She crouched and bashed her head against the frame. A kaleidoscope of colours fizzed across her vision, more than the impact, more than a hangover. She fumbled the key and shoved it into the lock. As she twisted the key, the door immediately opened inward. She lurched forwards, one hand grabbing the frame to prevent from falling.

A strained sunlight leaked into the hallway, washing over her.

"Tammy?"

Greg towered above her, dressed only in shorts. His red-rimmed eyes failed to focus. Still crouching, she felt as though the gloom pressed her closer to the carpet. She straightened but didn't get up.

"Where have you been?" His voice was soft, sleepy.

"Been downstairs. I—"

"I don't feel too good," he said.

Her legs refused to move. She dug fingernails into the frame, ready to pull herself up.

"I don't feel too good at all," he said again, and swallowed. "I ... I really don't."

She squinted up at him. Her knuckles whitened as she finally dragged herself to her feet, knees weak. She grasped the door frame, fearing she'd collapse if she let go.

"Greg?" she murmured.

Both his arms hung limp, resting against his shorts. The bandage. Dear God, the bandage. Blood soaked the once-white gauze to smear his shorts and drip down his leg.

"Tammy ..." His eyes rolled back in their sockets, lids flickering.

Behind him, a kind of fog seethed, obscuring the decor of the room. It was like smoke yet something more, swirling, thickening to block the sunlight beyond the curtains. The bed sank into the shadows. The wardrobe, the dresser, too. Everything. Plumes of grey and black churned. Smoke, smog, whatever the hell it was, the stench was salty like the sea, like something decayed. Rotten seaweed or something worse.

All that was left visible of the room was one wooden rafter. Only it stretched beyond the walls that were no longer there, spearing impossibly to the left and right, travelling for miles in both directions, off into the broiling darkness.

Greg stumbled back, arms out, and blood from the bandage peppered her cheek.

She blinked and reached out for him.

"Greg!" Her cry was snatched into the cloying atmosphere.

Her perception warped. Somehow he was further away, standing in the middle of what was once the room, with the back of his head near the wooden beam.

The sour taste of too much alcohol and this escalating insanity prevented her from speaking. She tried but it was like she'd swallowed sand. She grunted, feeling her chest tighten. Still she clutched the door frame, damp beneath her grip. Rivulets of moisture trickled down from the ceiling, tracing the woodgrain. Higher still, that fog drifted along the cornice, curling with the woodwork. Black patches sprouted like mould, splaying across the wallpaper.

Beneath that, the plaster broke through, tearing the paper, spitting dust and debris.

Nothing made sense. Here she was, out on the landing peering into what had been their room, where now only a dense fog existed. And that impossible wooden beam.

"Greg ..." she whispered.

The wood beneath her grip softened and split, and splinters tore her palm.

Her scream echoed to fall dead against the encircling darkness. She staggered and her arse smacked the balustrade behind her. She felt it give, just a little.

It snapped; a sharp crack, loud, ear-piercing.

Gravity tugged her.

Yet ... slowly.

Arms flailing, hand stinging, she grabbed for something. Anything. She grunted, cried out ...

Wisps of fog spiralled around her fingers, coiling like tiny phantoms, while all around her wood and plaster and brick wrenched apart. Tendrils of that thickening fog burst up with jerking floorboards, shredding the carpet. The walls cracked and crumbled, vanishing into the arms of the enclosing darkness. Where were the stairs? What the actual fuck?

From the smothering fog, those tendrils – more like goddamn *tentacles* – whipped outward and snatched her bleeding palm. Hot agony lanced up her arm. She screamed.

Her body jolted.

Suspended. Hanging with an arm upright while the incorporeal fog-shit snaked its way beneath her skin. Pain flared, raged through her. Her mind reeled and incredibly she managed not to black out.

She spun, rising, surrounded by that churning darkness. The final shreds of carpet and wallpaper, of balustrades and brickwork vanished into the fog.

Up she went, approaching Greg.

Both his hands and forearms were dark with blood, the tendrils pulling his arms up, outstretched and spreading his chest wide. He still stood in front of the wooden rafter that reached outward, defying physics in both directions.

Her scream, muted by the fog, burned her throat. Those foggy tentacles burrowed further into her skin, splitting the skin from palm to wrist, tugging free her veins and severing them. Her head swam in its own black void, threatening to take her down. Now split and torn, those veins linked with the fog, stitching them together, weaving and knotting. Her entire forearm gaped wide, skin flapping and spewing blood. It showered her face, her tongue. Coppery and bitter.

She kicked, she flailed, she screamed.

Greg.

Framed by the writhing fog which now looked more like a grey sky hinting of a storm, he rose upwards, his chin on his chest, hair drenched. His torso shone, slick with blood, now more black than red. The tendrils pulled his arms even wider, his muscles flexing beneath that glistening dark sheen. Both wrists gushed, blending with the swirling fog. Several probing dark coils tugged out his veins, just as they had hers. They snatched him fully up and wove sinew and shreds of flesh to the wood, lacing his veins together with tight black knots.

His legs swung, bloody splashes dripping off into the shadows that curled at his feet. His head lolled.

Did he move? Was he still alive?

Screaming, Tammy flew forwards, velocity snatching her closer to him. Moisture dampened her face as fresh pain blazed through every inch of her. She thrashed against those wispy tendrils, desperate for release.

Her veins wrenched free, spitting blood, severed.

Such incredible agony.

And she dropped.

Falling, she clutched her ruined forearm to her chest. Given that she'd witnessed the carpet and floorboards uproot, she expected to fall forever. But no, her feet thudded to the floor and the fog rolled up like waves. She'd lost one shoe. The carpet squelched between her toes. Cold.

She stood, looking up at Greg hanging from the rafter. Crucified, for God's sake.

From the far right, something snatched her attention. She squinted. Something pale, scurrying upside down along the beam, cumbersome, lethargic almost. Someone – naked? – fat, with flesh wobbling.

More some*thing*, grotesque, slick with glistening skin. Although obese, its limbs clung long and awkward around the rafter, clambering, inverted with jittery movements. Its head was little more than a bulbous mess of lumpy flesh and random thickets of hair. The closer it got, still Tammy couldn't make out any feature. Closer still, and she saw only a pair of eyes, green, intense … but from beneath the skin, glowing.

Her stomach twisted. Its gaze seemed to fire straight into her, burrowing to the core, to see who she was, *what* she was, to understand her very private thoughts and fears and secrets. It laid bare all that made Tammy the person who she was today. Indeed, what she'd become today.

It scrambled towards her husband, now little more than thirty yards away.

"Greg!" she yelled. She tried to step forward, her muscles straining against what she could only imagine quicksand to feel like. It tugged her legs, securing her.

It was even closer, its fleshy folds wobbling and shiny with perspiration.

Her ravaged forearm absolutely killed her, and she cradled it tighter. "Greg!"

She heard a deep rumble, a growl – a *purring* like a cat, really? – and it strengthened the nearer that thing got. The flesh along its flank rippled, the patches of hair bristling.

She had to do something, anything. But she had nowhere to go, still unable to move. Yet she couldn't leave Greg. And bloody-hell-fucking-shit did her arm hurt.

In the creature's wake, strung out way behind it along the rafter, vague outlines of people shimmered. A dozen or so ghosts. Men and women and even children hung from the beam, some bound to the wood with both hands, others with only one, their veins stitched with snaking darkness; all now little more than suspended skeletons covered in torn rags, stained and mouldy. Strips of shrunken, leathery flesh clung to skeletal limbs, and wispy hair hung loose from mottled skulls.

Still that doughy lump of a monster dragged itself towards Greg. Still Tammy couldn't budge.

More hung ghosts or whatever-the-hell-they-were appeared, strung along the wooden beam. Hundreds taking shape, solidifying, becoming sharper, more focused, more real. A whole line of them stretching off into the distance.

That obese nightmare was now almost upon Greg.

"No!" Tammy yelled, her voice hoarse.

Finally the monstrosity reached him and with one arm extended, flesh trembling, its fingers lengthened into bony claws. It swiped his chest, tearing loose the pec muscles, peeling away half his chest, nipple and everything.

She screamed, watching the huge strip of flesh come free in a red mist. His body swung, limp. He didn't react. Already dead.

Tammy's heart wrenched, churning like the surrounding fog.

That insane monster pressed the dripping chunk of muscle against its heaving belly. That doughy skin seemed to absorb Greg's ragged flesh. Tiny dark strands of fog encouraged it, lacing it together, allowing it to blend with that foul skin.

Tammy's legs buckled, and she gulped, ready to spew.

She watched, helpless, as again that thing raked away another strip of his skin, and again it applied the bloody chunk to its own body. Again and again, more and more shredded flesh, each time moulding it like clay. It worked its way down his body, stripping piece by piece, every muscle, padding out its own body. Now bulkier, its movements were lethargic, its strength noticeably reduced as it tugged strands of his leg muscle.

Noises from Tammy's left made her look sideways, along the length of rafter.

More creatures.

These ones, she knew, would be for her.

They scurried along the wooden beam. Some balanced on top, others inverted, like bald monkeys lean limbed and agile. All were much thinner than the first, and swifter.

The fog swirled around her, energised perhaps by the approaching hoard.

Wet sprays splashed her face. She blinked and didn't want to look at Greg's lifeless remains.

Something tugged her cardigan, something behind her. She spun round, legs still held firm by the heaving fog, and she looked up …

Tendrils of darkness had thickened, pulling her upright. Its intention was evident: it was going to string her up to the rafter, to allow those creatures to skin her alive.

They were closer …

Clambering so damn fast.

Closer, closer …

Greg's glistening body rocked, spraying blood as still that obese creature stripped him bare. Its limbs were twice as large now, lumpy, dribbling blood between the stitched patchwork of flesh. It moved with robotic precision, tugging slowly at the remaining clumps of muscle and sinew Greg's shoulder.

The thinner creatures were now much nearer.

Only a matter of seconds.

The fog closed in, jamming her senses, a dizziness clamping her head.

The nearest creature slowed on approach and hunched, its flesh a milky translucence with veins wriggling and pulsing beneath. Ready to pounce and—

A white light surged around her.

She jerked, body straightening, jaw snapped shut to echo through her skull.

The creature flew backwards. Its gangly limbs cartwheeled, smacking into another of its kin. Both spun and vanished into broiling shadows.

Greg's body rocked to and fro. Torn pieces of flesh remained only in places; he was now just a ragged skeleton. The immense hulk of creature slumped beside him. Its meshed skin quivered, hanging in folds over the rafter. It was evidently spent, satiated.

Another burst of light, of energy, and her body warmed.

Hot.

She jerked and staggered, tripped over her feet.

And she crashed to the floor.

The fog swelled around her.

More light. Blinding.

White. Bright. A burning sensation tore through her chest. Her mind reeled, bile rising and she choked. She thrashed around. But it was as though she moved in slow motion. Her arms numbed. Paralysed?

Another surge of brightness pushed away the dark, blocking her view of Greg and those smaller creatures as they approached the red mess of his dangling body.

Again, a fire raged inside her chest.

The whiteness consumed her.

No sound, no thought.

No feeling.

Only that brilliant white light.

Voices chattered. Frantic ...

Shadows flitted around her, shimmering, but not in the fog. This was different.

"... With us." A lady's voice.

Dark, fuzzy shapes distorted the white expanse. Blurred colours churned, blending like watercolour paints.

"Stay with us." A lady in a green uniform leaned over her. Blonde hair tied back, wide brown eyes as urgent as her voice. A paramedic?

Tammy's cardigan was open, bra exposed, and beside her ... dear God, beside her ...

Chunks of skin, ragged and curled, leaked a crimson pool into the carpet.

She felt someone grab her head and elastic snagged her hair. A plastic mask was pressed to her face. Something hissed. She gulped clean air.

Another paramedic, a man whose furrowed brow proved his commitment to the job, bound her wrist with bandages white like those she'd nursed Greg with.

"She's lost a lot of blood," Greg said. No, it wasn't Greg who'd said that, it was the man, the paramedic.

Tammy glanced beyond him, at the mess that was once her husband. Just a skeletal mess of tattered flesh and glistening bone. Chunks of muscle and sinew lay scattered around him. Bloody handprints covered the floral bedspread. Her gaze drifted, focusing on movement across the room, through the doorway and into the landing. The lady, the owner of the B&B, had a hand to her wrinkled cheek, speaking with a policeman.

"That's when I came running upstairs," the lady said.

The policeman scribbled in a notepad.

Beyond them in the corner of the landing, up near the light fitting, one of those creatures – a demon, Tammy had no doubt – clung to the wall. Swirls of fog coiled around its featureless head. Its skin taut across its face, but behind the sheen of flesh, twin eyes, burning green, burrowed into her soul.

The policeman nodded.

And so too did the creature; a short, sharp movement, flicking splashes of darkness across the wall.

"Always in that room," the lady said, "always."

Those black flecks seeped into the wallpaper.

DOUBLE RAINBOWS

Rayne Hall

Gerard hurried down the spiral staircase of Sibyl's lighthouse, his shoes clanking on the metal steps. The blue steel hands of his Rolex showed 8.13. The tide had turned two hours ago, and he did not want to get his new boots wet as he hiked home.

The steep chalk path from the promontory to the seabed was slippery with smudge from the night's rain. The sea surface glinted like a diamond-sprinkled sheet, and the air smelled of salty seaweed. In the distance, gulls cackled and squealed.

His chest brimmed with pride at how well he had handled the situation. Breaking to your girlfriend that you would marry someone else required a delicate touch, especially if she was pregnant. At first, she had hurled reprimands. Then she had demanded that he leave her home. But the high tide already submerged the way out, and she had to let him stay the night. After a lot of coaxing and consoling, her rants subsided to sobs. Gently, he pointed out that as an artist, she was above conventions like monogamy and marriage, and that single motherhood was all the rage. When he assured her she would remain the love of his life, and promised to continue his Friday night visits, she had stared at him in wide-eyed wonder. By morning, she had clung to him with surprising passion.

Sibyl had amazing curves, flaming hair and a temper to match, vivid imagination but little practical sense. She refused to sell the dilapidated lighthouse to one of the wealthy buyers queuing for 'converted character properties', insisting she loved living surrounded by sea. Isolated when the tide rose twice a day, with only her paintings for company, she lived for Gerard's weekly visits.

Driftwood, whelk eggs and cuttlefish bones littered the low-tide seabed, and bundles of dark bladderwrack lay entangled like scorched spaghetti. As he skirted around chunky boulders, the smell of fishy seaweed grew stronger, wavering between fresh and foul.

Rust-brown shingle and splinters of flint crunched under his fast steps. He had three miles to cover before the incoming tide wet his feet.

In the east, the sun was already painting the sky a brisk blue, but in the north, a curtain of silver-grey rain still veiled the view. A rainbow beyond the promontory framed the lighthouse in bright glory. He squinted. Was that a second rainbow emerging inside the large one? Even as he looked, the faint hues strengthened. Two rainbows, two women – the perfect omen for his fortunate future. Sibyl had probably spotted it already. He pictured her standing at the large window in her round room, paintbrush in hand, plotting to shape the vision into a painting.

But Gerard had no time to linger and watch the rainbows grow, because the tide waited for no man. Everything about nature – the sun, the rain, the rainbows, the tides – followed complex rhythms, regular but never the same. All was calculable – he patted the tide table in his jeans pocket – yet never quite as expected. Atmospheric pressure, moon phases and such all played a role. Stirred by wind and swelled by the rain, today's sea was already higher than normal.

Waves swished and slurped and rustled across the shingle. He took firm, even steps past black rocks, across broken shells and white crab corpses. Water ran in thin streams between sand and stones, down the almost unnoticeable slope towards the sea.

Soon he would have both: a rich wife and an unconventional mistress. A fair man, he would give both women the attention they deserved, but this required skilful planning. Erica could not be relied upon to show the same flexibility as Sibyl; she might even expect to have her husband to herself. He had to show tact and not spoil her illusions. A job involving absences from home would help, preferably no longer in her father's employ.

At 8.22, he reached the mainland shore where cliffs towered like steep castle walls. Thirteen feet above, sparse grasses grew in cracks, and gorse shrubs clung to precarious holds. Below that, nothing found a grip on the stark rock face, nothing survived the high tide.

He had another hour and a quarter to walk on the seabed to the end of the cliff that lined the shore. The wind rose, whipped up waves and sculpted them into mountain ridges. Puddles filled, and water streamed into rock pools. With the hem of his shirt, he wiped the thin coating of salt from his spectacles, and squinted at the sea. The tide was coming faster than it should.

An illusion, no doubt, from a water level raised by wind and rain. Today's high tide was at 13.01, which meant the sea did not hit the cliff until 10.30, and then he would be past the inaccessible part and on dry secure land.

He checked his watch again, just in case. The blue steel hands on the silvered dial showed 8.28 as it should. A quick glance back revealed the bill already washed by water, the route he had walked submerged by the incoming tide. Only its tip, the rock with the lighthouse, still pointed like an admonishing finger out of the sea. The rainbow was now clearly a double, its colours sharp.

Ignoring natural laws, the water crawled closer, brushing the scattered rocks with angry lashes and frothy caress. Puddles filled and forced Gerard to take big strides from rock to rock.

He checked the tide table, ran his finger down the column for today's high tide. 13.01. He was right, and had an hour and a half to clear the rest of the cliff.

Was the sun supposed to stand so high at half past eight? All he knew was that it rose from the east. On previous walks, he had not paid it much attention. He always left Sibyl's place at low tide, which was a different time every week, so the sun was never in the same place anyway. Though the sun looked high, and the water was close.

What if his watch had stopped? A Swiss Rolex was supposed to be infallible. *Ticke-tac, ticke-tac, ticke-tac,* the watch assured him, and the minute hand moved another notch.

As the water's edge sneaked nearer, he scanned the cliff face for an escape. Surely there was some gap, some path, some stairs hewn into the rock? But he had walked this route on many Saturday mornings, and knew there was none. Thoughts and fears whirled through his mind, questions, worries and doubts.

A drop of sweat slid down his back, and another. Keeping close to the cliff, he marched faster.

Wall-like waves crashed and shoved sheets of white foam at his feet. Tendrils of panic curled into his stomach while gulls glided past in mocking calm.

A cloud blocked out the sun. The air chilled and pimpled the skin on his arms, even as the sweat of fear pasted the shirt to his back. To his left, the cliff stood smooth, steep, merciless.

Salty splashes stained his shoes, sneaked into his socks,

soaked his trouser legs. The drum of fear beat in his chest. With the watch pressed to his ear, he ran.

Boom boom boom, his heart thudded. The watch went *ticke-tac, ticke-tac, ticke-tac* above the hiss of the waves.

The water rose fast. Icy wet snaked around his ankles, his calves. Still the cliff stretched without end.

No one could have reset the watch except last night.

Sweet Sybil. So grateful, so forgiving.

The next wave slammed his chest against the rock with ice-cold force.

THE PENSIONER PIRATES OF MARINE PARADE

Jonathan Broughton

"Look sharp, Daphne, Hugo Marshall's arrived." Clarissa reversed her mobility scooter away from the window. "Now remember, don't say anything and look blank."

Daphne gazed into space. *In a world of her own*, thought Clarissa. Looking blank was as natural to her as breathing, though that had been a bit ragged these last few days.

"Follow me," Clarissa ordered, and she trundled out of her flat and headed for the lift with Daphne close behind.

The main reception was packed, mostly with young or middle-aged relatives who had elderly relations living in Marine Parade. *Vultures*, thought Clarissa, as she eased her scooter behind the throng. *Out to make a few quid from the misfortunes of the old. Just you wait till you're in your hundreds and need help. I bet euthanasia won't be high on your list of priorities.*

She spotted a few pensioners, the hopeless cases, those with extreme dementia, who didn't know the difference between day and night, no doubt dragged out to illustrate government policy.

She parked behind a wall of bodies close to the stage. A good spot, she could hear, and if she leant to the left or right, just see the stage. Daphne drew alongside and bumped a couple as she manoeuvred into position. They turned, angry and shocked, though when they saw Daphne and her clumsy steering they shook their heads and rolled their eyes in resigned despair.

A ripple of applause and the crowd hushed to silence.

"Good morning, everyone." Hugo Marshall, Hastings Mayor and Clarissa ground her teeth. He shone in the spotlight like an oily fish. His bald head gleamed, his grey tailored suit glistened, his black patent leather shoes twinkled and his wide smile beamed.

"I didn't expect to see so many of you here," he began.

Clarissa snorted. Really? Every street corner in Hastings, every lamppost, had been plastered with posters.

"Today," Hugo Marshall continued, "I am happy to announce that The Silver Dusk will be sailing into Hastings on Monday the 20th October."

An appreciative murmur from the crowd and the couple in front of Clarissa turned to each other and smiled.

Hugo Marshall's voice adopted a considerate tone. "Do you have an elderly relative ready to die? Are you struggling financially to meet their upkeep?" Then, more strident. "Are you tired of resources being squandered on members of society no longer able to look after themselves? Inconsiderate individuals who took advantage of medical breakthroughs in the first two decades of this century to prolong their lives, but didn't consider the means needed to support their advancing years and who now rely on you for their care and well-being?"

A chorus of assent rumbled around the room.

"I thought so."

Clarissa wanted to smash her fist into his smug face.

"Well," he went on, "the expert team on The Silver Dusk can help. No funeral expenses, no costly cemetery upkeep. Do you know, and I speak from personal experience here, they are wonderful." His voice went low, almost husky. "My mother was so grateful when I took her on board. She was a burden, emotionally and financially, to the family and of course to the country. She understood that and chose the correct course of action. I shall never forget that last happy evening." His voice cracked and a single tear slid down his cheek. "Sitting in their Starlight Suite playing Scrabble. The lovely attentive staff helped mother choose the letters, and the memory of those final wonderful hours lingered when we came to say our goodbyes the next day." He took a deep breath. "Do you know, they even let us float the paper bag with her ashes in out to sea."

A whispered 'ah' rose from the crowd.

Bloody bastard! thought Clarissa. *I'd give him triple word score with bells on!*

Hugo Marshall cleared his throat. "Look around you, see the hopeless, helpless ravages of old age. These poor souls are incapable of making the right decision, but you, you can ease their pain. Join me at midday on The Silver Dusk and help your loved ones sail away to a golden sunset. The first five customers will receive a thousand pounds in cash."

Applause greeted his promise of money, but he hadn't quite finished and the crowd went silent as he delivered his final line.

"I care about the elderly. Do you?"

There were cheers and whoops of approval. Clarissa glanced at Daphne and smirked.

~

Clarissa steered her mobility scooter into the sea. "Look sharp, Daphne. Operation ROPES is go!"

She glanced in her side mirror to watch Daphne drive down the concrete breakwater. As the front wheels of her scooter splashed into the surf, she applied the aqua lever and the air cushion inflated as the fan booster whirred into life behind her seat.

Clarissa banked sharp right to line up beside her friend and breast astern, they bobbed up and down on the swell.

"Have you remembered to bring everything?" Clarissa asked. Daphne's memory slipped a lot nowadays, or chose random moments to be selective. Today's operation required concentration and keen wits. One error might find them both belly-up in the briny.

Daphne unclipped the bright red plastic picnic-hamper in her front basket and peered at the contents.

"Checklist," announced Clarissa. "Faces?"

Daphne held up two latex masks. Gross caricatures of old men with huge warty noses, tufts of long white curly hair and cauliflower ears.

"Pistols?"

Daphne grunted as she lifted the yellow and pink fluorescent water guns, moulded as AK47 rifles, into her arms.

"Loaded?" queried Clarissa, though Daphne's red face as she cradled them against her chest made it pretty obvious. Still, Daphne squeezed the yellow one's trigger and a jet of water shot across the sea and sent a paddling seagull skywards with a loud squawk.

"Good girl," congratulated Clarissa. "And ROPES?"

Daphne dumped the water pistols and slid two short poles, wound with black velvet, out of the bottom of the picnic hamper. She unfurled one to reveal a skull and crossbones and the slogan *Respect Our PEnsionerS* emblazoned across it in bright red darning wool.

"Perfect," Clarissa purred.

The sea mist rolled over them and onto the shore in waves of moisture. No breeze and no sign of the mist thinning. It never cleared, not since the earth had warmed up and melted the ice caps. The sun glowed like a yellow metal disc that gave no warmth and very little light. The calm grey water might be ice, it was so smooth. Excellent conditions for piratical exploits.

"Give me one of them dear," ordered Clarissa.

Daphne handed her one of the flags and she slotted it into the right-hand mirror bracket. Daphne copied her and they were almost set.

"Synchronise watches." Clarissa rolled up her cardigan sleeve. "Eleven twenty-five precisely."

Daphne's watch slipped upside down on her bony wrist and Clarissa reached across and helped her twist it back.

"It's hard to tell what that says," Clarissa grumbled. A grinning portrait of Hugo Marshall filled the watch face. "An airbrushed earlobe past a piggy eye. Well, it looks near enough, it'll have to do."

She checked her battery charge dial. The arrow flickered just under full. She glanced across at Daphne's, which looked identical. Now that the time for action had arrived, her stomach tingled.

"All right, dear. Now, The Silver Dusk is moored just off the old pier. Hugo Marshall is due to leave the harbour at eleven forty-five. We need to get into position between The Silver Dusk and the harbour."

This was their most audacious pirate attack yet. The thought of all that lovely money fired Clarissa's enthusiasm, which she tempered with moral sensibilities.

"We're doing this for Hugo Marshall's mother," she announced. "We didn't know her, but she didn't deserve to die. Come on, Daphne, raise anchor and *Yo Ho Ho* and a bottle of rum!"

She engaged her gear lever and eased in the accelerator. The fan booster whined and the scooter slid across the water. The flag unfurled and flapped as she picked up speed.

"Stay beside me," she called. She didn't want to lose Daphne in the fog and the wake from her scooter might bounce her out of her seat.

The old pier's rusty legs loomed out of the mist to her left. A red light blinked on the last piece of twisted metal, an excellent pointer to keep them on track and she pushed her accelerator to maximum. Poor old pier. She remembered the fire that destroyed it in 2010 and the earthquake of 2030 that tipped the remains into the sea. All that fuss about re-building had been a waste of time and money. What had happened to all that money? Nobody said.

The arrow on the compass next to the battery dial wobbled as it hovered over south.

"No room for error, dear," she called. "We're on our own now. Due south until we bump into The Silver Dusk and then north east towards the harbour."

The fan's whirr sounded so loud in the murky silence. The sea slapped against the inflated cushions. She and Daphne might be the only people on earth. The fog provided excellent cover, though it could prove treacherous if they steered off course.

Clarissa shuddered. Each year during bad weather pensioners went missing, presumed swept out to sea, after the earthquake opened the ravine that split Hastings in two. Tragic tales of mobility scooters spotted floating in the shipping lanes that criss-crossed the English Channel, their batteries dead and more often than not, their occupants too. To attempt a rescue was never contemplated, one less mouth to feed, one less expense for upkeep. It took pensioners like her and Daphne to make a stand against the authorities. *TAR*, she thought, *Third Age Revolts*. Good acronym for partisan activities.

"Look sharp, Daphne." She decreased the accelerator and her scooter slowed.

A dark mass loomed before them, as high as a cliff and as solid as a wall. Clarissa's heart thumped, The Silver Dusk, the death ship. No portholes broke its uniform bulk and thick fog obscured its upper decks. Silent and still, even the sea had turned a darker shade of grey.

She signalled left with her arm. She didn't dare speak because a horrid thought that, somehow, this floating executioner might be watching, kept her silent.

Then, with a blast that sent her nerves into orbit and the dreaded horror that her fears had been realised, the ship's foghorn shattered the silence with one long *boom*. If death had a voice, this might be it and she whimpered with shock.

Daphne's scooter collided into her and sent them both into a spin. They circled like wasps trapped in a jam-jar of water, until Clarissa reached across and yanked Daphne's accelerator off. They drifted away from The Silver Dusk until it was little more than a huge smudge in the fog.

Clarissa breathed deep to quieten her nerves. Her ears pounded with rushing blood, which to her alarm, increased in volume. She held her breath, it wasn't her ears. The sound came from all directions, the deep throb of a powerful engine as it churned through the water.

Flee! her mind screamed, but which way? Any direction might be wrong. Daphne's blank face gazed at her as she waited for instructions. Clarissa peered into the fog and her scooter trembled as it vibrated with the building noise.

The fog swirled and parted between them and The Silver Dusk and a golden motor-boat, high-prowed and sleek, slid past in a majestic sweep before the fog closed in and obscured it once more. The wash rolled towards them and sent them careering up and down, as sick-making as the worst rollercoaster.

"That's the boat that takes the victims to the death ship," Clarissa whispered, when she had recovered her breath. "Thank goodness it didn't spot us. You all right, dear? That was a nasty shock."

Daphne's tiny hands glowed white as she gripped her scooter's handles.

"It's off to the harbour for its first pick-up," Clarissa reasoned, and a terrible thought popped into her head. "I do hope Hugo Marshall doesn't come back on board. It's too big for us to tackle. I didn't think of that. Oh well, we'll have to wait and see." She laid a hand on her friend's arm. "Be prepared to abort the mission if I tell you to, dear."

She engaged the reverse gear and disentangled herself from Daphne. The compass needle trembled as the scooter completed a slow circle and lined up pointing north-east.

"Back on course," confirmed Clarissa. "Off we go."

She didn't know how far they might need to travel, just as long as they were out of visible range of The Silver Dusk and the harbour wall. She checked her watch, eleven forty.

"Two more minutes," she announced, "and we'll be in position." The fog horn boomed once more and she jumped with fright.

"For goodness sakes," she growled. "If the lethal injection doesn't get you, stand next to that and you'll be scared to death."

Daphne's blank face registered surprised concentration. *Bit like a worried sheep*, thought Clarissa. *I do hope she's up for this.*

The fog seemed if anything thicker. Her hair and face were soaked with damp and her palms slipped on the scooter's plastic handles. She checked her watch again.

"Ten seconds," she called and slowed the scooter to a gentle three miles-an-hour. The digital seconds flicked by. "Three, two, one, stop!"

She engaged the gear to neutral and the fan wound down and clicked to a halt. Daphne's scooter slid across the water and with a gentle bump, lined up next to hers.

"Open the hamper," Clarissa instructed. "Have the masks handy, but we won't put them on 'til we know what we're up against." Daphne handed her one. "If that big gold boat comes back, turn round and head out to sea until it passes."

Daphne angled the water pistols with their hilts uppermost for a quick and easy draw.

"Just typical if Marshall decides to show off and travel in style," worried Clarissa. "Hey up, what was that?" She listened hard. "Do you hear it?"

A gentle *phut phut phut* echoed through the fog.

"I think we're in luck, my love," Clarissa grinned. "He's coming out in his fishing boat, just as I hoped." The inboard motor came closer.

"Masks on," she ordered. The cold latex stuck to her wet face and the rubber smell made her wince. She pushed the mask's bushy eyebrows out of the eye sockets. Next time she would give them a good trim. She grabbed hold of the pink water pistol and laid it across her lap and then patted Daphne's hand.

"Quick in and quick out, remember?" The leering old man that faced her, nodded.

Clarissa engaged the gear, gave a thumbs-up, and eased the accelerator to maximum. The scooter shot forwards and the flag streamed beside her like running water.

Within seconds the tiny fishing boat jumped out of the fog in front of them.

"Avast there, yer' scurvy dog!" yelled Clarissa. She swerved to the right and Daphne swerved to the left.

Clarissa locked her knees under the scooter's handles, picked up the water pistol and pumped rapid jets of water across the boat's deck as she swept past. Daphne repeated the action on the opposite side.

Hugo Marshall, easy to spot in his scarlet regalia and gold chain of office, jumped up and attempted to shield his robes from the soaking by raising his hands as if he might push the water back.

Clarissa cleared the stern the same time as Daphne. She gripped the scooter's handle with one hand and yanked it sharp left. A quick glance behind her confirmed that Daphne had remembered what to do as she turned sharp right.

Lined up on opposite sides off the boat, they made another pass. Jets of water arced through the fog and Hugo Marshall's hands waved and flapped as one demented.

"Give us the money," shrieked Clarissa.

Through the boat's cabin window, a young man's face glowed green. Law dictated that all vehicles, except mobility scooters, be fitted with satnavs and, to Clarissa's knowledge, every single one of them shone with a green light. The man's eyes stared in wide disbelief at what was happening and as she and Daphne swept past for a third attack, the boat's speed decreased, until it sat and wallowed in the swell left by their scooters.

"Pincers," Clarissa shouted. She aimed her scooter in a direct line at the boat's port side as Daphne did the same on the starboard side.

"Give us the money, Marshall." Clarissa heaved the pistol onto her shoulder, squinted through the plastic telescopic lens, which had no glass but two bits of bent wire for the crosshairs, and hit the Mayor in the face with a spray of water. He cursed and spluttered and shouted obscenities. Daphne aimed for the back of his head. Spray rebounded in a dazzling display, like a glistening halo.

Clarissa's scooter bumped against the boat's side. There, at Hugo Marshall's feet, floated a large metal case. It gleamed with a silver shine. The money!

"Hand it over," she commanded and squirted his drenched face with another burst.

The young man slipped and slithered out of the cabin.

"Do something," gurgled Hugo Marshall.

Daphne focused her aim on the floundering youngster and he lost his footing and crashed face first into the bottom of the boat.

"Give it to me," Clarissa growled. "Or, by Davy Jones's locker, you'll take a swim with the fishes." Water sloshed in little wavelets round the Mayor's feet. He raised one arm to protect his face and, with the other, reached under his sodden robes.

"Keep your hands where I can see them," Clarissa shouted and pumped his chest in a series of staccato bursts. Daphne left off drenching the young man and copied Clarissa's tactics on the Mayor's back. The power of their ferocious bursts, the weight of his soaking robes and the waterlogged boards underfoot, unbalanced Hugo Marshall and he crumpled in a scarlet heap like a burst balloon.

As he fell, his foot kicked the metal box and sent it aquaplaning towards Clarissa. She stood up, leant over the scooter's handlebars and hooked the box's handle with the barrel of her water pistol. It was hers, all that lovely money and she dropped the box into her basket.

"Scatter," she called to Daphne, as she engaged the scooter's reverse gear and drew away from the boat.

Daphne looked up, as lost and wondering as a lonely child.

Clarissa's heart sank. 'Not now, Daphne, don't blank out now.'

"Engage, Daphne," she shrieked. "Scatter, scatter."

Daphne watched without the slightest flicker of awareness as the young man lurched to his feet. In his hands was a rope and attached to the end of the rope was a large hook.

"Get out of it, Daphne." Clarissa flicked into forward gear and swerved towards the boat's stern.

With a loud clunk, the man hooked Daphne's handlebars and pulled the rope tight. The noise, or perhaps the man's close proximity, jumped Daphne out of her stupor and her booster fan whirred as she pulled away.

The man braced his feet against the boat's side as the rope tautened. His face strained with the effort of holding on, but the rope slipped through his hands and he let go with a loud yelp.

Daphne's scooter jumped back with a splash. Clarissa closed with her and reached for the hook, but Daphne engaged forward gear and accelerated away.

"Daphne, the hook, get rid of the hook." She chased after her friend. 'What was she doing? She'd be tipped into the sea when the rope played out its length.'

"Slow down," she yelled.

Daphne's bent little figure hunched over the handlebars and her speed increased. She swerved in front of the boat's prow and sped past port side towards the stern. She swerved again, up the starboard side and the trailing rope, slicing through the water with a *hiss*, wound round the boat.

Clarissa gave up giving chase, going round in circles made her dizzy, and when Daphne shot past she saw, in her eyes, a look so grim that it made her gasp. Daphne's mind was clearly fixed on one thing, though what that might be Clarissa couldn't guess.

The young man crawled into the cabin. The lurid green glowed on his face as zombie flesh in a horror film might look. The boat's engine sputtered as he gunned it into life and then it whined with a high-pitched squeal, followed by a loud clank as it cut out.

Clarissa chortled. Daphne had jammed the propeller with the rope. Clever girl! Now she could clear the hook and leave Hugo Marshall stranded at sea.

Daphne decreased speed and turned her scooter to face the boat. She went into reverse and the rope tightened, wringing water drops. She glanced at the instruments on her handlebars and as Clarissa watched, she lined up in the direction of The Silver Dusk.

"Daphne?"

The fan booster whirred to full acceleration and Daphne moved backwards into the fog, her face beaming with joy and the fishing boat followed, slowly picking up speed.

Clarissa's scooter rocked in the gentle swell. She suddenly felt very lonely out on the ocean, her victory over Hugo Marshall, hollow, almost worthless. In fact, everything was pointless because, when she thought about it, everyone died and whether it was helped along by a smiling nurse with a lethal injection or the carelessness of being carried out to sea in bad weather, didn't matter. Death happened, happy, sad, or ordered. It took courage to make a deliberate choice and she marvelled at Daphne's resolve. She didn't think the old girl had it in her.

Her maudlin thoughts evaporated when her eye caught the gleam of the metal box and her heart gave a little jump. It might all be pointless, but pointless in style. No point dwelling on sad thoughts, not when there was money to be spent.

The fog turned orange, an explosion, muffled but deep, followed by the high-pitched whistle of a ship's alarm.

Clarissa lifted the flag and waved it in triumph. The Pensioner Pirates of Marine Parade had struck again and she laughed at the fog, gave the metal box a loving stroke and blew Daphne a last fond kiss.

AWAY IN A MANGLER

Mark Cassell

Overhead a rusted bell clunked, a muted announcement, and Tanya stepped into the narrow shop. Glass ornaments on mirrored shelves rattled as she closed the door behind her. Winter's bleached sunshine lanced from a row of delicate swans; subtle rainbow colours twisting with the moulded glass, tracing their detailed anatomy. She wiped rain from the tip of her nose and strolled further into the shop, aware of the wet squeak of every other footfall. She suspected the sock was wet but couldn't quite tell through cold toes. A smell of cinnamon and furniture polish washed the cold air from her nostrils.

There were no other people in the shop called *Looking Glass*, and even the wood-panelled counter was void of a proprietor. Beside a battered yet evidently cherished 1950's till, a squat Christmas tree twinkled fibre-optic branches. Glass snowflakes hung from several limbs and a winged angel sat at the top, again glass-sculpted. A yellow halo wrapped around its head above a pair of wide Japanese anime-style eyes.

From plastic superheroes to replica broadswords, greeting cards to wooden board games, this was the kind of place you'd find something for everyone. One corner which leaked into a window display was dedicated to Christmas.

Among glass sculptures of snowmen and robins, of reindeer and the all-important baubles, a glass nativity scene took precedence beneath fairy lights. The manger was the only thing not to be made of glass, instead matchsticks crisscrossed one another, and cradled in a tuft of real straw was a glass Jesus complete with white nappy. Tanya doubted they'd had such brilliant white linen two thousand years ago, but she guessed there must be an artistic licence in glass sculpting.

Voices drifted from a back room. A woman's, croaky but not in an elderly way: "We need more."

"Christmas is fast approaching," replied a man's voice.

"Just go shopping." The woman's voice rose higher. "As soon as possible."

"But—"

"Today!"

Tanya glanced back at the display in the window, at the handwritten sign exclaiming 'Job Vacancy, Apply Within.' She tugged her bag tighter over her shoulder and stepped towards the door, her boot squelching – all that rain to remind her she needed new boots. But she didn't want a new boss who yelled like this. Having left London for a quieter life, she'd quit a demanding job with a high salary and a bastard boss, and here she was looking—

"Just do it!" the woman shrieked.

The man's voice was low and Tanya couldn't quite make out what he said.

"I don't care," the woman concluded.

Her previous boss she'd told to shove it, and should anyone speak to her like she was now overhearing, she knew she'd do the same again. She'd moved down here to the south coast, to this quaint seaside town to escape the bullshit. She wanted a job – *needed* a job given that the little money she had remaining was tied up in her new home –

but listening to the argument behind the closed door …
yeah … perhaps this place wasn't for her.

Tanya's hand was already on the door knob and she
peered through the glass, out into a street of bustling
Christmas shoppers.

From behind her, the man said: "May I help you,
young lady?"

She paused, muscles tense and she glanced again at the
sign in the window. She could just about see it between the
glass globes – paperweights, she guessed – their centres of
swirling colour, churning dark rainbows that reflected the
cold sky outside. The way a pair of them were angled, they
reminded her of eyes. She turned on her squeaky heel.

A man perhaps in his late-40's stood behind the
counter, the door behind him creaking closed. His stoop
made him seem old beyond his years, and his eyes flashed a
friendly hello. He tugged on his lapels almost comically and
straightened as much as his hunch allowed.

Again she glared towards the sign in the window.

"Um …" She needed this job. The newspapers were
empty of local vacancies, and the other shops in town
already had staff. This was the only available job nearby and
she'd never learnt to drive.

"You're here about the job vacancy?" the man asked.

She nodded and released the handle, and her feet
moved before she realised what was happening. He looked
up at her as she reached the counter. A toothy smile
cracked the man's face in two and wrinkled it further.

"Good, good," he said.

"I was wondering—"

"Have you worked in a shop before?"

"Yeah, a few years ago while I was at Uni, I—"

"Do you live local?"

"I've only just moved to Winchelsea, wanted to escape London." Using the word 'escape' made it sound silly but was kind of true.

It was his turn to nod. "Can you start today?"

"Um…"

"Now?"

She looked behind the man, at the frosted glass door and wondered where the woman was. Had she been standing behind the counter beside him, Tanya knew she'd decline but instead she replied, "Sure. Why not?"

"Welcome to our tiny team." He extended his hand. "My name's Mr Kennedy."

His calloused grip was firm.

"Tanya," she said, "Tanya Green."

"Well, Tanya, I have some errands to run and you starting now would be immensely helpful."

"Of course." She felt herself relax. She assumed this man owned the place and perhaps his wife who remained out back was the boss, too. Tanya thought if she could answer only to Mr Kennedy then all would be okay.

"We open every day of the week, nine till five-thirty. Your hours will typically be 40 a week, but you can have more. Or less. We can all be flexible, I'm sure. These days I can't run around as much as I'd like." His brow creased and his eyes drifted along the shelves. "We've always sold this kind of thing, altering stock according to the season."

"They're wonderful," Tanya said and stepped towards one of the many mirrored shelves. Like the window display, the sculptures twinkled beneath a row of fairy lights: a dragon, a row of scorpions, even a Pegasus. This last had always been her personal favourite as a child – who didn't love the concept of a flying horse?

"I glass sculpt myself, you know." He straightened up, defying his rounded shoulders. "We've a workshop at home."

Numerous glass snowmen mingled with fantasy creatures and domestic animals. A military tank and a tractor stood out between a pot-bellied Father Christmas and a detailed fireplace complete with hanging stockings. All delicate glass, some large, others tiny, each containing subtle swirls of colour. Beautiful.

"Come, come," he waved her around the business side of the counter. His gold wedding ring was tarnished.

For the next five minutes he explained how the till worked and how to complete card transactions, where the paper bags were and how some stock was beneath the counter.

"Finally," he concluded and opened the frosted-glass door, "through here is the loo."

She peered round the scuffed doorframe and into a small hallway, seeing a chipped and peeling door labelled 'WC' and a threadbare staircase leading up into a dark red gloom. Up on the landing, heavy curtains covered the wall. Daylight leaked around the edges creating a wavy pattern.

"However," Mr Kennedy added, his voice rising slightly, "please do not go up there."

Tanya assumed upstairs was their private rooms, yet a moment ago had he not said his workshop was at home? She wondered where his wife was and desperately wanted to ask. Maybe she was upstairs right now. Wherever the woman, Tanya didn't actually want to meet her.

She eyed Mr Kennedy as he allowed the door to creak closed. She didn't know what to say. Thankfully, the front door of the shop juddered open and the bell clunked. The sound of wet tyres hissing on tarmac followed the entrance of a lady with a young son. Closing the door behind her, the lady walked into the shop and glanced around. The kid wore a bobble-hat far too large for him.

"All yours," Mr Kennedy said to Tanya and stood in front of the glass door. He nodded at the till.

"Morning," Tanya said and dropped her bag beneath the counter, beside a stack of white boxes with the word 'December' lazily scrawled on the front. Apprehension tugged her stomach, familiar with any new job. After all, she'd entered the shop herself no more than ten minutes ago.

"Shout if you need me," Mr Kennedy whispered, "I'll be upstairs."

She watched the pair wander round the shop, eyeing stuff. After a few minutes they left without purchasing anything. During the next couple of hours, several customers came in and soon her first sale of many was a snowman; the little girl whose father bought it barely contained her excitement. Eventually, footsteps down the creaking stairs reminded her that Mr Kennedy was around—the job was so easy she'd forgotten about him—and he came through the door. He squeezed past her, a faint whiff of plastic and something else, perhaps oil, following him.

"Any problems, Tanya?" he asked. He wore an overcoat, green and creased.

"Nope, all good. Sold a few things, mostly glass."

"Always glass." He beamed. "I'm off out for supplies."

The rest of the morning passed and a considerable amount of cash and card purchases went through the till. One of the glass dragons went to an older gentlemen who paid more attention to the military tank, strangely. Tanya guessed the dragon was for a grandson. Come lunchtime, she wondered what she was going to do about food. Hunger pangs had already attacked her and she was convinced the last customer, a man with a scarf that covered most of his face, had heard her stomach. It had rumbled louder than a passing truck.

Not only that but she needed a pee.

The shop was empty. A quick dash to the window to look up and down the street showed that it too had quietened, so she hurried to the loo. She was quick, all the while her ears strained for a familiar clunk of the bell. Luckily nothing. As she went to enter the shop again, a scraping sound from upstairs made her pause. Her palm pressed on the frosted glass door, cold, but she didn't move. It had sounded like something dragged across floorboards.

Thump.

Tanya's heart leapt, and she swallowed. Whatever it had been, it was certainly something heavy.

Thump-thump.

Mr Kennedy had told her not to go up there, but what if Mrs Kennedy was in trouble? Perhaps she'd fallen over and needed help. Already, Tanya's boot was on the bottom step.

Thump-thump. Thump.

She charged upstairs. On the landing, she turned a sharp right and the red drapes swept with her. For a moment, daylight washed along the hallway and sent vertical spears of shadow up the wall from a dozen balustrades. Then the light shrank back. She stopped, heart in throat, before the first door she came to. Another stood in the gloom at the end of the hall.

Silence, save for a heartbeat pulsing in her ears. And her breath, short and sharp. She dared for there to be more sounds, more thumping noises. Yet nothing. Maybe it had been from behind the other door.

"Hello?" Her voice, that one word, seemed somehow brighter than the gloom. She leaned closer to the wooden panels. The paint – white, yellow, she had no idea; difficult to tell in the weak light – flaked in places, curled patterns with the grain beneath. About to step away and head for the other door, she heard something. Maybe … Yet she couldn't quite tell. Was that shuffling?

Yes.

Again, a thump.

She grabbed the round handle and twisted. It slipped in her palm and she tightened her grip, pushed inwards. She squinted into the daylight from a window across the room. Such was the glare, what occupied the room remained a silhouette between antique furniture. A chair, and in that chair—

"Oh my God!" Tanya lurched forwards and crouched in front of a woman not much older than herself, bound with silver duct tape. From behind what looked like a grimy tea-towel used as a gag, the woman squealed. Muffled, desperate. Dark hair clumped across her forehead, flopping into her tear-reddened eyes. Her cheeks were pink, moist. She rocked in her chair. Thump, thump. Thump.

A sweet perfume washed over Tanya as she first yanked at the woman's restrained wrists, and then her ankles. It wouldn't break, she needed something sharp. A knife. Anything sharper than her stubby fingernails.

Another muted cry from the woman.

Tanya assumed this was who she'd heard that morning, with whom Mr Kennedy had argued. Was this Mrs Kennedy? Surely not; too young. This could be the woman Tanya had replaced. Or perhaps even their daughter? Tanya realised the man hadn't actually mentioned a wife. Although he did wear a wedding ring. All these thoughts, like lightning.

She slid her fingers round to the back of the woman's head and pulled at the gag. The woman groaned. Her hair was tangled with the knot, tight, and Tanya failed to undo it. Again she tugged the duct tape.

"I need something sharp," Tanya told her.

The sideboard and dressers were covered in doilies, and one was bunched beneath a silver tray. Nothing sharp in sight though. About to straighten up and look properly, Tanya saw the woman's eyes widen. Bloodshot with green pupils, large and round and they focused on something over Tanya's shoulder.

From behind her, Mr Kennedy said: "I do wish you'd not seen this."

Tanya's breath snatched in her throat. She went to turn, and ... bright, heavy pain burst up her neck. Into her head.

And darkness crashed down.

~

Jolt and a jerk. Motion. The sound of an engine rumbling, roaring, gears shifting.

Huddled almost foetal-like, Tanya's senses overlapped beneath a pressing throb at the back of her skull. Her shoulder jarred something hard. A darkness still wrapped around her, tight over her eyes, blindfolded, and her mouth was forced slightly open by what she guessed was a fucking tea-towel like the other woman. Her wrists were taped behind her back, her ankles also bound, tight and pinched.

Another gear change. The smell of oil mingled with a familiar perfume ...

So she was in the boot of a car and wedged against someone else. The other woman, it had to be. Where were they being taken? Who was this other woman? Tanya's breath hissed through her nostrils, the gag hot and wet.

Dark. Motion. Heat from the woman – unconscious? Dead? – beside her. Soon ... soon the car coasted to a halt and the engine was cut.

Tanya's gut twisted.

A door opened. Slammed. Footsteps scraped gravel, and the boot lock clunked open. Cold air flooded over her.

"Glad you're awake," Mr Kennedy said. She heard and felt a swipe of a blade, freeing her ankles. Calloused hands grabbed her and she was up on her feet.

She screamed into her gag.

"At least I don't have to carry you," he said. "But I am ever so disappointed."

Her heart punched her ribcage. Her breath threatened to choke her, louder than the pummelling headache. She wanted to run but being blindfolded, she knew that was ridiculous.

He shoved her in front of him. "Move."

She staggered on legs of jelly for several metres and then her boots sank into whispering tufts of grass. Where were they? Her arms ached, twisted behind her back at an awkward angle. Eventually they stopped. Her head spun. What was he going to do to her? Kill her? Rape her? In that moment, she couldn't think of what was worse. A chain rattled and something – a padlock? – thumped against wood. A door juddered open. Nudged from behind, she stumbled over a threshold. The darkness of her blindfold suffocated her more than the gag. They paused as he pressed some switches. Click, click-click. Click. Then a solid mechanical clunk of a larger switch echoed, and a great engine hummed. The way it reverberated from a distance suggested the place was sizeable and she imagined a farmyard barn or something. Indeed, wherever this bastard had taken her, she could even smell hay, grease and diesel fumes, perhaps even the heavy stink of animals.

Again, she hollered into her gag, which increased her headache.

She grunted. Even in darkness, she saw flashes of colour. His fingers dug into her arms and together they shuffled along. The further inside the building, the stronger the smell of diesel fumes and the louder that rhythmic hum of a machine. Things crunched and scuffed beneath her boots and she imagined treading on bits of wood and screws and perhaps even broken grass. Another door screeched open and this, she knew, was where the machine was. It was as though she'd entered a factory of some kind.

Several more metres of darkness, and finally they stopped close to the rattle and roar of some sizeable machine.

A woman's voice shouted, "Tie her to the chair!"

It was the same woman who'd yelled at Mr Kennedy earlier, the one Tanya assumed was his wife. So whoever was in the boot wasn't who he'd argued with. Or was it? To reinforce her confusion, she hadn't even been aware that someone else was present. Light and shadow pulsed across her vision. None of this made any sense. Who was in the boot? Who were these people and what were they going to do?

Those rough hands pushed her down into a seat and the hard wood bit into her arse. Again, she screamed a muted scream, and the tearing fabric sound of tape being unwound made her swallow it. Again, her ankles were fastened only this time to chair legs.

"Such a shame," Mrs Kennedy said, "such a shame."

Tanya's heart hammered between her ears, somehow louder than the clanks and shudders of the machine. Metal on metal and scraping, grinding; it filled her head, throbbed with her headache. Someone shifted her chair and she jolted sideways, and they snatched off her blindfold. She winced, averting her gaze from the bare bulbs high overhead. Blinking, she focused on—

Dear God, what the hell was this?

Supported by great chains from rafters, a series of rusted machines and tarnished panels stretched between one corrugated wall and another. A squat tractor, like something from the 50's, shuddered atop concrete blocks. With its wheels removed, the rear axle spun a well-greased chain into the rattling belly of what she assumed was a combine harvester or hay bailer. Between that and a number of bolted panels, the chaotic motion of wheels and cogs and pulleys led to a platform about knee-height and rimmed by a number of jagged blades. Each jerked and slid against each other with a cruel *ka-ching* sound that enhanced the machine's echo. Below those blades, a ramp tilted downwards towards two immense stone wheels. They slowly turned, grinding together beneath another juddering engine. Black fumes belched from between several loose panels. At the end of this absurd contraption, a funnel gaped over a dented bucket from a mechanical digger.

From behind Tanya, the woman's voice drifted over her shoulder: "Proud of this."

Tanya tried to shift round, to look at her captives, but Mr Kennedy's hands clamped down on her shoulders.

"Keep her there," the woman said. "She can see what's going to happen to the other girl."

Tanya wrestled again, straining against her bonds; the duct tape digging into her wrists and ankles.

"Stay …" Mr Kennedy clamped her shoulders. "… There."

"Or she'll be first into the machine." The woman said and shrieked laughter.

Tanya's mouth went dry.

"And she'll be the first out," added Mr Kennedy and released her.

Not even daring to move her head, her breath whistled from her nostrils, rapid. A coldness ran down her spine, out into her arms and legs, freezing her fingers and toes. She heard footsteps retreat and assumed Mr Kennedy had now left them to bring in their other captive. That means she was still in the room with the woman – whom Tanya still thought of as Mrs Kennedy. Whoever she was, Tanya didn't want to aggravate her. Though Tanya hadn't even met the woman, she pictured an older lady whose grey ponytail pulled sharp features into a bug-like glare.

And Tanya felt those eyes burning the back of her head.

Still the engines roared.

Her sobs rocked her body. But she fought to keep still. She wanted to turn to look at Mrs Kennedy, she wanted to scream, she wanted to run. She did not dare.

Several minutes passed and a commotion from the doorway snatched Tanya alert.

It was Mr Kennedy hauling the other bound woman over the threshold. Straw and mud covered her clothes. She shuffled along almost tripping them both, and it was all the man could do to keep her upright. Her yells, muffled by the gag, rose in pitch when she saw those clanking blades. She wasn't blindfolded.

Still the machine hummed, the chains rattling, and diesel fumes chugged in billowing clouds.

"Come on!" Mr Kennedy shouted as he struggled with the frantic woman, heading towards the platform. He leaned against a vibrating panel, gasping. His fingers like claws dug into the woman's arms and heaved her onto the ledge.

The woman's eyes widened, inches from the glinting blades, and she shrieked and kicked back – for an insane moment Tanya eyed the shoe and admired it – and the heel scraped down his shin. He grunted and shoved harder, and she almost fell from the ledge. He rammed her all the way onto the platform. A part of the mechanism snagged her shirt and yanked her arm into the hungry blades. The surrounding panels shuddered and for a moment the lights dimmed, then surged. Her muffled yells turned to screams as the great machine thumped and banged and dragged her into those chomping metal teeth. The sound of metal on metal now became a rhythmic wet slicing sound, heavy, meaty. Blood pooled and oozed from the platform, soaking the straw at the base of the machine.

Tanya's heart ran as fast as her breathing. She closed her eyes tight. Darkness so welcoming but it only managed to heighten the sounds around her. The woman's muted screams, and the blades ... the blades making that wet, cutting sound.

Thump-thump-ch-ching. Over and over.

Teeth clenched, eyelids clamped so tight it almost hurt, and in that darkness the rhythmic thunder of the machine filled her, pumped through her, rattling her bones. Those blades sliced, meaty and mushy. In the smothering black void behind her eyelids, the stink of damp, of choking diesel fumes, of grease, stole her senses. And that thumping, that goddamn endless thumping, amid the constant sound of grinding stone ... and now trickling and slopping meat. She didn't want to – she couldn't – open her eyes.

Mrs Kennedy, further away and behind her, laughed. A shriek of delight and she even fucking clapped, the crazy bitch.

Tanya thrashed in her chair, bile rising up into her gag. Somehow she swallowed it down. The machine shook, rumbling through the floor while she listened as more meat slopped into the bucket. Finally, reluctantly – she had to see what these mad, mad bastards were doing – she opened her eyes. The gloom filled her and it took an incredible amount of effort not to look at the machine, at the slowly grinding millstones at the end of the contraption. She didn't need to look; she knew they glistened red.

She peered over her shoulders expecting to meet the so far unseen woman, but no. Mr Kennedy approached.

"Miss Tanya," he said. "I honestly do wish you hadn't discovered your predecessor."

Was it her turn next? Sickness boiled in her gut and a billion thoughts crashed through her head. Tanya pitched sideways to see over her shoulder. Then the other. She couldn't see his wife. Where the fuck was she?

Mr Kennedy grabbed her head and pulled down the gag. It rested around her neck, soaked with spit, as she gulped for air.

"Let me go!" she screamed at him.

"We can't let you go," he said ... but this time in a different voice.

"Wh—" Tanya's vision blurred, the criss-cross of overhead rafters, the juddering machine, Mr Kennedy's twisted smile, everything shifted as he spoke in another voice ... a *woman's* voice.

"Shh," Mr Kennedy said, this time in his own voice, "you've confused her."

"Doesn't matter either way," the woman said through his lips, feminine yet croaky. "She's material to us."

"What the fuck?" Tanya shouted.

The man shook his head. "You shouldn't have seen any of this."

"What do you want from me?" she demanded.

"You!" It was the woman's voice again.

Mr Kennedy walked behind her and pushed the chair towards the platform. Blood still dripped from the ledge.

The chair legs scraped the floor, juddering and vibrating through Tanya's body.

"No!" Acid boiled in her gut. "Don't do this!"

The woman's voice: "We must."

"Yes," Mr Kennedy added, "this is unfortunate."

Raw clumps of flesh and bone and torn fabric flopped around the blades. Flecks of blood and chunks of filth splashed in all directions, some peppered his trousers.

Tanya felt some dampen her forehead and cheek. She winced, again fighting bile as it clawed up her throat.

Mr Kennedy stood over her, beside a dented panel that was missing a screw. Its rusted, jagged edge rattled. He held a Stanley knife, thumbed open the blade and crouched in front of her. With a flick of the wrist, he freed one ankle and then the other.

She braced herself and with both feet, booted him in the chest. The knife flew from his hand as he slammed into the concrete blocks beneath the machine. On her feet, kicking away the chair, she immediately backed up to the loose panel, fumbling for the jagged corner. She awkwardly lowered herself to rub her bound wrists against it. Pain, warm and slick, as the metal tore her skin and thankfully the tape.

Mr Kennedy came at her on all fours, and reached out, lunged forwards. She ducked and fell sideways into the machine, her wrists still bound but looser. Her head smacked the machine and something like camera flashes momentarily blinded her.

"Come here," he said and then in the woman's voice, yelled, "Grab her!"

He clutched her and she desperately twisted her wrists to free them. All the while he wrestled her closer to the millstones. The stink was strong. A crimson mess churned from the funnel, rolling out and slopping into the bucket. It peppered up the sides of the vibrating metal.

She kneed him in the bollocks.

He released her and doubled over. The woman's voice shrieked from his mouth, "Bitch!"

She rammed him with a shoulder and he staggered backwards.

Finally, she tugged free her wrists. The tape flapped as she swung a fist into his face. Something cracked, blood exploded from his nose and he scrambled along the ledge with one hand. The other held his face, blood oozing between his fingers.

With palms flat, she shoved him onto the platform.

A millstone caught his hand and yanked him round. The engine groaned. He shrieked – the woman's shriek. His forearm went in further, *crack*, *crunch*, and his whole arm followed. His screams smothered Tanya and she backed off, watching his legs fold. The machine whirred and shook amid an intensified groan from overhead. Still pieces of the other woman's body clung to various parts of the machine as it fed it through down into the quivering bucket.

Those massive stones shuddered as they turned, snatching his upper body. Angled, his neck bent backwards and a final scream echoed as his jaw tore free and then hung for a moment, along with his tongue now caught in the gradual rotation. The great millstones stuttered then continued. A grey purple mess popped through his skull as it bubbled and spat crimson, crunching it flat, wrapped in torn clothing and mangled flesh and bone. The surrounding panels rattled and shook, and a slick crimson mess oozed down the funnel.

Tanya backed away on legs that threatened to give way. Vomit scratched a bitter exit and filled her mouth. She spat, tears streaming, and she turned and ran, stumbled and almost fell. She made it to the door. Her hands still sticky with her own blood, she grasped the handle and twisted. She looked back.

A great belch of black diesel fumes rushed out from the rear of the machine and a suspension chain snapped. The engine shifted, tilted, and a panel popped off. It clattered across the floor in a pile of hay. An overhead rafter dislodged, splintered as gravity snatched it. A sheet of corrugated roof followed, and both crashed down. Another rafter split. More fumes choked the air.

Mr Kennedy's legs kicked as though the fucker was still alive, and the millstones pulled the last of him into the mangled mess of fabric and flesh.

Tanya tore her gaze away and lurched towards the exit. Her mind reeled, seeming to turn like those millstones. Again, she wanted to spew. On unsteady legs, she made it into a corridor lined with stacked cardboard boxes. Several propane bottles, almost as tall as her, stood near a doorway that led off into another room. Her pace was slow, but it was all she could do not to collapse, and she peeked into the adjacent room. She saw a table with some kind of burner fixed to the surface – it reminded her of the Bunsen burners used in science lessons back at school. Glass rods lined a bench, some of varying colours. She staggered past. Then slipped. She fell sideways into the boxes. The contents rolled out, making a tittering sound as several knocked together. Her knees smacked the floor and she watched the glass baubles roll towards her exit.

Huddled and shaking, she listened to the machine in the other room create renewed crashing noises. Yet all she could do was stare at the spilled contents.

She tasted blood and vomit, and the clogging diesel fumes burned her throat as she gasped. She clenched her teeth, grunted, and pushed herself to her feet. Her hands were as red as the mess that had churned from the millstones. She stumbled for the door. Slick, slippery fingers managed to open it. Next, she was outside.

A smouldering sunrise touched the tops of trees.

She staggered past Mr Kennedy's car. Along the gravel drive – one step, another, and another – out onto the road.

Even though the barn, that insane building was way behind her, she swore she still heard the thundering machine, grinding, bones cracking, crunching. And the mess, the curdled red and green and purple mess, the shredded clothes, the chunks of mashed flesh and bone.

And the boxes. The stock.

Had she not been referred to as "Material"?

The walk back into town took her far into the morning, and she cared little for the looks some people gave her. Early-morning dog walkers for the most part … But she didn't really see them. It was all about one foot in front of the other. She knew where the police station was.

Finally, she made it. Up the steps, her boots still squelching, blood streaked her clothes – God only knew what the hell she looked like – and she made it into reception.

A Christmas tree stood proud in one corner, tall and green and covered in decorations. She recognised some; similar to those in the shop and to those she'd knocked over in the barn.

The police officer at reception looked up and jerked upright, and then she said something. Tanya failed to hear because of the sound of that damn machine thundering through her head. How could she still hear it? All this way back into town and she still heard it.

Thump-thump-thump. And the crunching bones, squelching and oozing clumps of meat.

Footsteps, someone was running towards her. To help? She was okay now. Safe … But …

Dark spots clouded her vision. Her head swam. Still the machine shuddered inside her head.

She toppled forwards, arms like rubber, clutching air.

The tree toppled and she crashed to the floor. Inches from her face was a bauble. It rocked back and forth, and came to a rest beside a piece of chewing gum mushed into the worn carpet. Inside the glass, she wasn't surprised to see pieces of fabric twisted with the swirls of colour, of red and green and purples. Bone shards, too, if she really squinted.

Grind-shudder, and crunchcrunch, crunch.

The police officer's boots jogged into view, and Tanya wanted to say how nice they were but her lips couldn't form the words.

Still the great machine thumped and clanked and roared between her ears.

ABOUT THE AUTHORS

JONATHAN BROUGHTON writes fantasy, horror, paranormal and urban stories. Any story in any genre in fact, depending on the idea or the plot that pops into his head.

For many years he lived in Hastings on the south coast of England and all of the stories in this anthology were written when he was by the sea.

As well as the short stories he has also written three novels. A thriller set in Victorian London at the outbreak of the Crimean War, a modern-day crime investigation that takes place in Hastings and a fantasy, also set in the East Sussex area, *In the Grip of Old Winter*.

In the fantasy, eleven-year-old Peter travels back in time to ten-sixty-six just after the Battle of Hastings. Intrigue and confusion blossom as the local population adjusts to life under the guidelines laid down by their newly victorious conquerors. And in the woods and the hidden places, old magic reawakens. It is hard for Peter to know who he can trust in this strange time and the decisions he has to make then impact on events in the past and in the present.

Many of Jonathan's short stories have been published in Rayne Hall's *Ten Tales* books and April Grey's *Hells...* series.

He has worked as a Poll Clerk and a Presiding Officer for various local and general elections, an examinations invigilator and as a puppeteer in theatre, films and television. He now lives in the University City of Cambridge, UK.

www.amazon.com/author/jonathanbroughton

www.facebook.com/jonathan.broughton.5

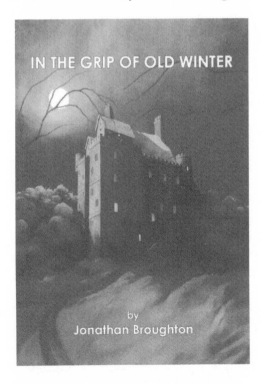

MARK CASSELL lives on the south coast of England with his wife and a number of animals. He often dreams of dystopian futures, peculiar creatures, and flitting shadows. His jobs have included a baker, a laboratory technician, and a driving instructor, and 2018 sees him acting in the horror movie *Monster* directed by Matt Shaw.

As a familiar face on the UK convention scene, Mark sells his books as well as his photographic art, and doesn't charge for selfies. The busy man that he is, he also hosts writing retreats for Writers' HQ.

Primarily a horror author, his steampunk, dark fantasy, and sci-fi stories have featured in numerous reputable anthologies and zines. His best-selling debut novel *The Shadow Fabric* is closely followed by the popular short story collection *Sinister Stitches* and are both only a fraction of an expanding mythos of demons, devices, and deceit. The novella *Hell Cat of the Holt* further explores the Shadow Fabric mythos with ghosts and black cat legends.

The dystopian cyberpunk collection *Chaos Halo 1.0: Alpha Beta Gamma Kill* is in association with Future

Chronicles Photography where he works closely with their models and cosplayers. He's often alongside these guys at conventions all around the UK, and one of their shoots inspired the creation of his new Lovecraftian steampunk horror universe that begins with the novelette *In the Company of False Gods* available on Amazon.

www.markcassell.co.uk

RAYNE HALL writes fantasy, horror and non-fiction, and is the author of over sixty books. Her horror stories are more atmospheric than violent, and more creepy than gory.

Born and raised in Germany, Rayne has lived in China, Mongolia, Nepal, Britain and Bulgaria. For many years, she resided in St Leonards on the coast of East Sussex where she penned many creepy stories, including the tales in this anthology.

Rayne has worked as an investigative journalist, development aid worker, museum guide, apple picker, tarot reader, adult education teacher, bellydancer, magazine editor, publishing manager and more, and now writes full time.

You'll find free creepy horror stories on her website, and writing tips and photos of her cute book-reading black cat on Twitter.

www.raynehall.com

twitter.com/raynehall

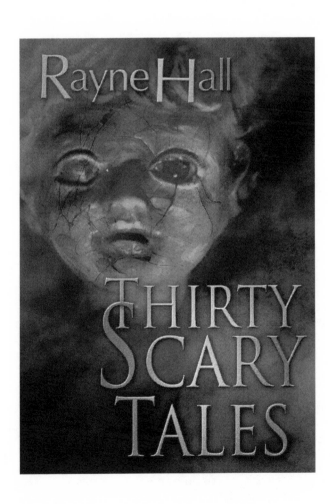

And finally, this book would not be complete without a nod and one huge **THANK YOU** to our cover artist ...

REDSKI REDD is an East Sussex based photographic artist specialising in beautiful, strange and spooky artwork.

Redski takes his inspiration from the charms that he finds online and in Hastings, Rye and Brighton antique and charity shops. In his photography studio, Redski turns everyday items, toys, and models, into stunning and unique photographic artwork.

He also creates original book cover artwork for horror novelist, Mark Cassell.

www.redtownphotography.com

For your FREE story go to:
www.markcassell.com

HERBS
HOUSE

Made in the USA
Columbia, SC
05 February 2018